PERSONAL
ACHIEVEMENTS

Francisco Javier Morales Ercambrack

historiasjm@yahoo.com

CONTENTS

For my high school and university friends, for those of the various jobs I've had, and for those friends that without intent have given me the joy of their company.

Personal Achievements is the translation of my novel written in Spanish called Logros Personales. Alice M. Woodrow translated it and Pamela Erin Mason revised it for the 2022 edition.

I
MY FIRST JOB

"The boss's word and promises are never trustworthy," Omar told me with firm conviction once he and I, as office mates, gained confidence in each other. We both began to work for the government at the same time in what, many years ago, was the equivalent of the current Ministry of Economy. Our boss was Jaime, who was then the sub-director of God knows what. Socrates, "The Politician," had recommended Omar to Jaime, and a university professor recommended me. That was my first job. I was lucky to get a part-time schedule, which helped me finish my Bachelor of Arts degree, earn money, start to dream, and see what the future held for me in terms of money. At that time, I had no ideas in my head about professional development, saving for retirement, or seeking a balance between family and work life.

I remember that I started to work by drawing graphs. I was given the data of interest, from which I extracted the proportions and then drew the graph in pencil. Afterward, someone else made them with ink, and the product was photocopied and appended to a report. At that time, micro-computers didn't exist. Another activity of mine was to search for data on the topics of interest to make charts that would reflect how a particular sector of economic activity was doing.

The problem I was facing was that the information was scarce and probably low quality. I think nobody knew anything at all, but everyone told you they were aware of everything. Besides, all my acquaintances had important and high-paying jobs (although sometimes they asked me for money loans), and soon, if everything went well, they all would end up having managerial jobs.

At that time, when I was a bureaucrat, luck smiled at me, at least on a work level. With my first check, I bought the complete works of Alfonso Reyes, which I still have at home unopened. With subsequent checks, I was able to cover the expenses that I incurred for having my first lover. To say the latter would be to show off about something that, in a strict sense, was not true. The lady, whose name was Victoria, was the one who wanted or needed to have sex, and I happened to be near (at hand) and at her disposal. Come on, the woman was pretty, curvy, and attractive. Also, one likes to imagine that one can do more than what one can do and that everything is rosy. This made me think, in the beginning, that my affair with Victoria was as easy as pie. I was happy. We made love at all times. Once, we escaped a weekend to Cocoyoc. For three days, there was sex before breakfast, at noon, after lunch, before and after drinking tequila, when coming out of the shower at night and, if we were still bored since we barely spoke, Victoria and I would cheer up again and practice the famous game of "put in and pull out" of *A Clockwork Orange* until we were completely pleased, asleep in each other's arms. By this, I mean to say that, while it is true that I didn't wake up in her arms, as the song goes, I did fall asleep around them.

The first night, I was full of joy because of the turn that my sexual life had taken. I felt, as Woody Allen would say, that I should have practiced these topics by myself. I think Victoria was enchanted. At that moment, if someone had proposed an operation to elongate my virile member, I swear I would have gone into the operating room immediately. Today, I would be more cautious because someone told me the story of an Arab genius who appears to a macho man who asks him to have a penis so long that it would reach the floor. The genius, according to the story, doesn't think about it twice, and *Bang!,* he quickly cuts the poor individual's legs off.

"Master, now your sex reaches the floor just like you ordered," the genius says while bowing respectfully. Inside, that faithful servant is happy about having met the wishes of his Master speedily and just as he asked. Well, no, thinking it twice, I think I better keep the original equipment with which I arrived into this world and thus avoid some traumatic misunderstanding. Besides, the genius or even the surgeon may know the side effects, which they don't share with the public for fear that the brave would become cowards; therefore, the clients might run from the treatment if they suspect that, with time, a small piece of the transplant could fall off, or that a permanent malfunction could arise. God! This sounds worse than Moctezuma's Revenge, where tourists get sick in the stomach after eating Mexican food, and when the rosy world quickly becomes one of sadness and dark skies.

Anyway, the second day in Cocoyoc was like the first. Luckily, at that time, I was in my twenties and, as of the nth time that Victoria and I were playing in the bed, I said to myself,

"Listen, Javier, be careful with that woman, may she not bruise that penis for life and the poor thing becomes useless, and not even works a little when you are older and you have to perform with other girls. What are you going to do if she leaves you with everything squashed and defective? And then, how will you fix that? Worse yet, who is going to fix it? I don't think that any tinsmith will repair it and leave it like new, right?"

I think that, as the surveys say, I was *a little* worried about that situation and I'm also sure, like the surveys also say, that I wasn't *too* worried about that problem. To what I understand, the difference between *somewhat* worried and *very* worried can be abysmal. Well, if I had been dismayed, now I think it was very little, barely, because Victoria and I were dedicated to playing with care to what very naughty girls and very restless boys do when they are alone and no one is seeing them and, between laughter and tumbles, they constantly play the little house game. I must confess that the last night I spent in Cocoyoc, when I was about to go to bed, I felt a little scared. When I placed my head on the pillow, instead of praying and commending myself to the Lord without asking for anything special for me, I said silently,

"My God, I cannot anymore. Give me the strength to close with a flourish this performance and to fully meet the worldly obligations I still have pending."

I felt like the "Little Big Man," which in his time was Dustin Hoffman when he had to sleep in an Indian tent with three amazing Sioux or Apache Indian women. They, through insinuations and smiles, required his sexual services.

The poor character, with decreasing efficiency and great effort, attended them all.

That night, I hoped that Victoria was as exhausted as I was and that she would be a good girl and go to sleep quickly. That did not happen. I don't remember the details, and not because, as it is said, I am a gentleman (the saying says that gentlemen have no memory) but because, even though no one believes it, I became autistic momentarily, just like those children who need special attention and mentally withdraw themselves from the world, particularly when there is a problem around the corner.

I think I complied with Victoria like I had to. Honestly, I may have a little fault or a slight lack of coordination here and there, and even perhaps I was a little uncontrolled, but I'm sure that in no case did the problem get worse. Once our bodies were separated, I thought about curling up in one of the corners of the bed and to start telling Victoria that one of my legs or knee was hurting (maybe my back, a vertebra, or something), just anything that I could invent to avoid having to play the "put in and pull out" game that night. I had my head on the pillow and was just waiting to be able to sleep like a log. However, things did not happen like that; being that, concerns came to my mind.

"Oh life, how complicated you are!" I told myself instants before closing my eyes and seeing whether this would lead me to rest. Instinctively, as if my body were left defenseless while I slept or tried to sleep, I put my hands on my sex. I don't know what was worrying me. I confess that any male in my committed situation would be scared a little and would have done the same. One only had to think of the possibility that Victoria would wake up very late at night and would again want to play the game that mothers and fathers play when they are alone. When seeing that the father didn't have the full impulse or the required energy, she would have applied her hands as sharp and electrifying pincers on my lower parts seeking a quick and satisfactory response from me.

"Oh, God! Protect me!" I meant to scream from the darkness and solitude of the defenseless corner where I was, when this terrible thought crossed my mind, like deafening lightning. For a moment, Victoria appeared in my thoughts, or maybe at the beginning of a dream, with her pretty face in the body of a fierce and overexcited lobster that moved its hard pincers with threatening dexterity, here and there, while it slowly approached me. Fortunately, a little time later, my eyelids dropped flat, and I slept like a well-behaved child.

I must admit that the sex feast that I had in Cocoyoc turned into indigestion, not so much for my genitals but for my blood pressure. In the beginning, I was all right, although down there I felt that the situation was not all that normal or optimal. I had a certain tickling that lasted some days and only disappeared when I applied diaper rash creams. I confess that my concern was authentic, and it would have become anguish if not for the quick healing of that essential part of my body. Just imagine, I would have stayed with a flattened part of my body and shattered self-esteem!

After the idyllic weekend that I spent in Cocoyoc, I felt bad the first day I was in office. I felt lazy and I was shattered. I would have bet that my blood pressure had dropped to the floor or, worse, that I didn't have any, like a recently dead body. When I least expected it, I fell asleep on my desk. I would have sworn that I only closed my eyes a couple of seconds, like someone does to recharge energy or to give oneself a brief breather, but Omar, my office mate, was the one who woke me up. Scared, I opened my eyes and I thought from the fright that the world was ending and that a crazy person was screaming in front of me.

"C'mon, idiot, open your eyes, you fool. You've been asleep for almost two hours, and if the boss sees you, he is going to be pissed, and with me too for being stupid and letting you sleep," Omar said to me scolding while shaking my arm with force. To date, I'm grateful for his considerate attention in waking me up. In retrospect, I'm sure that, thanks to him, I was able to keep my prestige as a compliant bureaucrat, attentive to my work.

"What's the matter with you, idiot? Do you feel unwell? You look shitty. Get up with that sloppy face you have, and go to the secretary and tell her that you want to leave the office because you are dying of pain. If she asks what hurts, you tell her that you have a pain in the balls that is killing you, and you tell her very seriously that if she wishes to see them, you will show them to her with pleasure," Omar told me with a big guffaw while pushing me toward the secretary.

So, that day that I felt bad I told Jaime's assistant that I had a fever and left the office before the closing time. At that moment, I considered myself a fortunate bureaucrat. I think that if I hadn't been working, Victoria, like any firm, would have considered another candidate to take my place, and we would never have gone to Cocoyoc. Nowadays, I sigh and tell myself with melancholy,

"Well, Javier, these are the things that one does in life and, in the best-case scenario, they leave you good memories. You just have to be grateful at all times that your penis was not damaged, not smashed either, and that for only a few days it was partially bruised on one side."

"In short, as the experts say, congratulations because after various serious squeezes to the testicles and after all the times that Victoria treated you hard and you felt the cord of your life, which also links you to it, was going to burst, you still came out of it. Fortunately, nothing serious happened, and you only returned weak full of rings under your eyes. Phew! Test overcome! Congratulations!"

Before completing one year in my job, I got sick with pancreatitis. From what the doctors told me, I was this close to being taken dead out of the hospital. I was seriously sick and, just what life is, my gall bladder was operated so that I could get cured. Once I recovered, I returned to work in the office to what used to be my usual routine. Then, I underwent other sad events that affected my emotional health. I went from a rosy world to one of horrible, deep, dark skies. In the meantime, Victoria substituted me with a guy some years older than me, named Manuel, whom she had just met at the Master's Degree school where she had begun to study. Frankly, I felt very emotionally pounded and on a downward trend—as happens in the stock exchange whenever there is one bad news after another—when she told me that I had fulfilled my cycle with her.

Never before had life hit me so bad and so hard, as when Victoria did. Much to my surprise, instead of a murderous lobster, Victoria turned out to be a street prizefighter who only knows how to hit low and place dry punches where it hurts the most. I should admit that this woman didn't tell me that my cycle with her had ended, but those words ring much prettier when they tell you the same in another way, or in a way that leaves you emotionally hurt for life because they destroy your self-esteem.

"Get out of here, Javier, I'm through with you. I don't want to continue looking at your sad dog's face, do you understand me?" is what she, more or less, told me with contempt one day that I went to her home without informing her. I confess that, at that moment, I felt disoriented, like an abandoned puppy on the street, that the cars are about to run over it. And indeed, I recognize it. I went to her house that day to try to get her to put on me the training collar and, if I was lucky, to pet me. I think that, on that day, Victoria didn't have a maid and she had to do some of the housecleaning. I suppose that this got her in a really bad mood and, unconsciously, she was waiting for the first fool to appear at her door to take out on him how ungrateful life can be. I also think that, for a great lady, it should be very depressing to be the Cinderella who has to wash dishes, clean the floor, and take out the trash, in short, to do all the things a mortal has to do when he or she is responsible for a home.

"You know one thing, you good-for-nothing? I don't want to go out with you anymore," she told me as a manner of greeting, the moment she opened the door and saw me. I think I was lucky that, at that moment, Victoria didn't spit on my face.

The rudeness of the words was too straight to not affect my mood. Then, Victoria stood there looking at me for a moment, as if my gaze had called her attention. She got her breath back, and instead of starting talking to me, she went straight on to inform me that things between us had changed radically. That is, Victoria made me understand that a woman of her level, of her category, and as good-looking as she was had to be free and that I had no entry in her life, in her projects, or in the stage of development she was experimenting at the moment. The truth was that, even though it was a little uncomfortable for me, she was not crazy or desperate about us dating.

By the hard look Victoria's face had when she saw me, I guessed that she wanted to tell me that the sooner I went to hell, fell off a cliff or into a drain hole, disappearing from her life, fast and quiet, just like that, as she snapped her fingers, the sooner she would be happier. I think—she never really told me but my non-feminine intuition made me understand—that she had fallen in love with her new boyfriend and that I had been discredited before her eyes because I had failed some important test that she had subjected me to. In my defense, I can say that, at that time, Victoria had never informed me that she had tested me. Later, at some point, I thought that it was possible that when I was with her in Cocoyoc, maybe I failed somewhat. I don't know if it was a mechanical issue or one of effective execution in the performance of my last loving act there. Maybe she didn't like something I did, or maybe she expected me to give her more than what I was able to do.

"Do you want to know something, Javier? I'm bored with you. You are only wasting my time. I see that with you, there is only sex, sex, and more sex. I'm sick and tired of you, and that you only think about that. Do you perhaps not know that a woman like me is only interested in love, in real love, that noble feeling that transforms you and makes you feel like the most fortunate woman in the world?" Victoria told me, then, a little surprised by the fact that I was next to her, she placed one of her hands on my shoulder in a soft but firm way, pushing me away from her.

"Besides, Javier, I don't think that I'll get too far with you. I dreamed about a honeymoon in Paris, walking hand-in-hand through the streets that skirt the Seine, full of love, illusion, and incredible projects, full of affection and tenderness. In that beautiful sentimental trip that I had imagined, my love and I would realize how our sentiments grew and turned into something colossal by just looking at the nightly lighting of the Eiffel Tower from the Trocadero and drinking champagne under the moonlight. But what happens when it doesn't occur? I only look at you, and I feel paralyzing idleness. I see myself degraded and badly dressed, asking for charity in the adjacent streets to the Seine. With you, I only have the disillusionment of having spent a miserable and boring weekend in Cocoyoc. Alas, Javier! Place yourself, please! Treat me like a lady should be treated—a high-class lady like me. Deep in my heart, I'm convinced that I don't matter to you in any way and that you have only been using me during this whole time to satisfy your insatiable macho man pride in bed," Victoria told me with annoyance, which I didn't know was real or feigned. Besides,

I perceived a tone of nuisance in her voice, which could have very well been destined for my person or to the wall.

From the attitude and expressions that Victoria used, I thought that she wasn't the same person that I had known or thought I knew. Despite the devastating impact that her words had at that moment on my spirit and my self-respect—because emotionally I was at the edge of the cliff—in an inexplicable moment of lucidity, I thought that I was watching an old movie by Maria Felix, perhaps one of her famous melodramas with which her disdain she would bewilder her husband, her lover, or—why not?—both, and if she had been able to be present at the movie theatre at that moment, even the spectators. In my mind, some scenes were running at a great speed, where this actress is disappointed in her lover, and he—that's me—is completely disconcerted and doesn't know what to say or do while, without knowing it, little by little the blood begins to flow again to his brain and he asks himself the following question:

"What is wrong with this good-for-nothing bitch, who in the twinkling of an eye has changed her pose and thinks that instead of a coarse cotton shawl cloth she is now wearing a mink coat? What was it that affected her brain if, deep down, she and I are from the same town, since we have always seen each other and chatted while standing in line for the *tortillas*, and every day we eat prickly pears and plain pasta soup at the diner on the corner, and not caviar or lobster Provençal at the most expensive restaurant in the Polanco area? Goddamnit! It is valid to say that I'm no longer attractive to her nor is she interested in me, but why all this ire and frustration, so as not to say hate and resentment?"

She looked at me attentively, and I think that she perhaps guessed that instead of feeling like a good-for-nothing, I was beginning to get angry. I saw that her gorgeous green eyes blinked too much. She gave me the impression that she thought for an instant just what she was going to say to me and then changed her strategy. Now, the tone of her voice and her attitude were less hostile and more amiable. She went from the hard and merciless character to that of an ingenious and tender negotiator. With sweet words almost dripping honey, she told me,

"Javier, my love, be good to me. I ask you please not to look for me anymore because you know what? My heart tells me that I can't continue doing things for you. I feel that in some way, you are pressuring me, and that makes me feel bad and sad. I feel that deep down, you do nothing but judge me in the most severe possible way, and I feel that you don't understand that the only thing I want is to give love unconditionally and purely. Please forgive me. I am a lady, and I will always behave with you as such, with care and affection. You are a nice memory that I keep in my heart as something highly esteemed, but from now on, I have to worry about myself and ask you and many other people to give me space, to have a lot of patience with me, and not to look for me. I can't give you any details, but right now, I'm going through sad and difficult moments that are forcing me to be alone, rebuild my soul, and find the light that will enlighten my way to try to be a better person. Also, I'm quite convinced that I'm entering a new stage of spiritual growth in which I have to concentrate all my attention and energy, and you have to help me by setting me free. Right, Javier? You will be good to me, and you will help me out by doing all that I'm asking you to do?"

Victoria said all that while she looked at me with utmost tenderness. Almost immediately, she came close to me and, with both her hands, she took my face, and with almost love, she caressed it lightly. I confess, that was a moment of total weakness. I think that deep inside, I forgave her and I shouted at her desperately, "Victoria, my love, I understand you, trample on me all the time your spirit requires for you to be in peace, but let's have sex now or in the coming five minutes." Fortunately, those words stayed stuck in my throat like a fishbone that suffocates us, because, before they could come out of my mouth, Victoria kissed me on the forehead, pushed me gently toward the street, and almost without me realizing it, closed the door on my face.

When she said the pretty words by which she asked for my support, she also looked me in the eyes. At that moment, her face overflowed with tenderness, and she no longer withdrew herself by pushing my shoulder with her hand. In the beginning, her tone was believable, although, unfortunately, a few seconds later, it began to sound a little melodramatic. Then, without her realizing it, she changed her tone of voice to a monotonous one, the same that comes out of us when we are talking and, at the same time, a long yawn escapes us, which we are too lazy to dissimulate because we are completely bored.

I was sad—so as not to say emotionally crushed or destroyed—from the way Victoria had expelled me from her sentimental life if she ever had such a thing. I realized that I had passed extremely quickly from the concern of too much sex to no sex at all. While I was recovering from that great erotic-emotional calamity, I dedicated myself to listening to Jose Alfredo´s songs, so they could give me a big dose of comfort and help make my life more bearable.

A few months later, luck smiled on me in the work life. That is, Jaime, my boss, was named director of God knows what. He asked Omar and me to change departments and to go with him to work as his assistants in this new job. What would we do, exactly? Who knows, but Omar and I agreed that if we wanted to improve our income and, why not say it, our career prospects, we should change our current job if the new one was better paying.

II
MY NEW JOB

My new job was an extension of the previous one, except that I began to work full time. Now, it could be said that Jaime proposed to Omar and me to be his helpers, although before, it would have been said that Omar and I went with him as his private servants. I think that the helper concept is a little more refined and elaborate, since it gives me the idea of teamwork, while the servant figure implies more personal achievement and more independent work, like what the damn cats do meowing excited on top of the fence of the house on the corner in the early morning without stopping. Maybe the cat meows are desperate screams with which it tries to find a cure for an ache that is crossing from side to side of its famished body. It is also possible that those meows full of pain were caused by another damn cat (Victoria?) that abandoned it, that told it that it didn't have an entry in that stage of its feline life, and to better go and lose one of its filthy seven lives in the depth of a cliff. Between the meows that torment those who are sleeping and its contracting heart every time it breathes, the sad cat feels that the damn female has ruined its life forever.

If one damn time you can't sleep, are fed up listening to the wretched feline of the block, and decide to hurl a stone at it in the middle of the night, don't be surprised that every time you succeed in hitting it and knock it down, it falls standing–like a good politician–scratching and hurting everyone around it. That's the way damn cats are: individualists, unpredictable, treacherous and, of course, one has to recognize it, of great personal achievements. Also, one does not have to attack a miserable cat just for fun, which, as also happened to oneself, has also experienced a great heartbreak.

In the new job, they promoted me, and I had to make forecasts about the Mexican economy. The tasks consisted of obtaining the series of data needed to forecast and other variables considered relevant. We had to fill some sheets with these data and take them to another office to the data entry clerks so that they would codify datum per datum, card by card. Once that material was ready, we had to take it to the computer center. There, we delivered our perforated cards and then had to wait a while. In that lapse of inactivity, Omar and I checked out the secretaries of that place. The secretaries—maybe because they were more mature than us or because they wished to have the attention and favors of other males with higher hierarchy and better salaries than us within the bureaucracy—didn't pay any attention to us.

At the end of the day, the IT people would return some sheets to us with the results of the estimates launched by the computer, and we would abandon the place somewhat frustrated because none of those girls had responded to our euphoric greeting. But we weren't completely disappointed because we knew that we would return the next day and, of course, would try our luck once again with those girls that seemed to be not too friendly.

Once we had finished our work, Omar and I returned happily to our office. On the way, he talked about politics, and I listened very attentively. I tried to understand and learn why someone hated another, who had stolen what, who joined a powerful bloke or so-and-so, who was being mentioned to get such and such a position in the public administration, who and why had fallen in disgrace, and if one was more corrupt than so-and-so.

Then, Omar would expound on his hypothesis on why Luis had named José, José named Miguel, and Miguel named Carlos. If I was in touch with Omar now, I know that he would have new hypothesis and conjectures and he would tell me why Carlos, once he repented having named Luis, corrected his error by naming Ernesto, and why Ernesto had no choice but to twiddle his thumbs. He would also tell me why Vicente had been so mediocre, and why Felipe gave mixed signals of being confounded and not knowing how to distinguish between the good and the bad and, in addition to that, why Felipe had preferred to help Quique more than Josefina.

During the years that Omar and I were fellow workers, I thought that all that he told me was no more than the visible flesh-and-bones face that the powerful Mr. Money from high school had in real life, particularly in the country's politics. Also, Omar's comments made me realize that life had put us all in constant competition to earn one's bread and butter (bring home the bacon) and try to make it up day to day or week to week so that our families can have sustenance. Omar's words, summarizing, allowed me to see how our work turned into money (i.e., each day's money).

"All politicians, dude, are fucking bastards. They will always tell you things they are willing to swear on their mother's tomb but, of course, they never comply. Do you know why? It's simple because the prostitutes that gave them birth repented of having done so and swore by all means and in all the brothels where they have worked that they were not their mothers. And those poor souls grew like that, like little trees rocked by the wind here and there, with no mother, no ethics, no nothing," Omar would tell me, very serious, every time we ended a conversation on this topic just as we were about to reach the office building. We would not talk about politics anymore until the next time we were walking down the street.

Omar, with the cautiousness that characterized him when he talked about these things, once told me,

"Don't be a fool, if the boss hears you talking about politics, he is going to think that you want to screw him, because he will immediately think that you are only going down the hallways intriguing, looking for his dirty and long-tail just to give it a mighty stomp or to cut it with something that will hurt him very much. One day, he might see you with bad eyes and he even might get furious and, for being a fool, he could hurl a blow with his tail that will beat the hell out of you, and without realizing it, you will be left without a job in a twinkling. And, if the rumor runs that you dared to confront the boss, you're in trouble for life, because, then, no one will want to hire you or employ you, even if you asked for a starvation wage. In case you didn't know, the maxim in the bureaucratic world consists in obeying the boss, and to do otherwise is the worst sin, so as not to say affront, that one can commit. In brief, Javier, as the insignificant bureaucrat that you are, you are obliged to obey, genuflect, flatter the boss, and lick his boots among many other denigrating activities. And watch it, never dare to think on your own, because, if things don't turn out as the boss wants, you will be screwed up. Thus, as you well know, don't be dumb by opening your mouth and repeating what I just have told you, do you understand? Because, of course, they'll come after both of us if someone finds out that we had this conversation, and that we have questioned our bosses."

Omar ended this long, tiresome speech by looking me in the eyes. I suppose he wanted to be sure that I had gotten the message.

In the beginning, the new job was somewhat fun, but over time, it stopped being so, for two reasons. In the first place, because the computer center was on the 14th floor of another building and one damn day, when I was alone up there, waiting for the results of my computer runs, a strong earthquake struck the city.

"Son of a…, mother…," I thought about shouting all these words like a crazy man, while I became pale with fear.

I had never been worried about an earthquake, but frankly, it is not the same to feel a building moving with force from here to there when you are four meters from the ground than when you are at forty. The building went from left to right with force, like a fragile boat would do on the high seas amid gusts of wind and high waves. At times, I could see from the window how I was coming close to the sidewalk. The earthquake and the fear made me first imagine how my body would fly out of the building and fall on the pavement. Then, according to my catastrophic thoughts, a mountain of debris would fall on top of me.

"Poor me," I told myself in silence to avoid other people thinking that I was a miserable coward, just at the moment when I took refuge under a beam with others whom you could see were more frightened than I was.

"Here I disappear from this world and my sad and not too useful life ends when a stone breaks my head and many other bones," I told myself again in silence while the building continued to sway. At that time, it was clear to me all that one had to do in one's work life to earn sustenance honestly.

The second reason why the new job lost part of its enchantment came when things became urgent, and this happened frequently. In that situation, everything was getting complicated, and it didn't matter if it was raining or snowing, if a celestial fire was falling from the sky, or if a damn union blocked the streets. Omar and I were in a building, and the computer center was in another, three blocks away. Thus, an important part of this stage of my life at work went by me having to run from one building to another.

One day, it was pouring rain, and I had to take the perforated cards to the computer center to get some urgent new forecasts. I returned to the office, dripping water from all sides and very upset because I had fallen into several puddles and my shoes and socks were sopping wet. That day, I was so angry and unmotivated that I called everyone "Bastard!"—the boss, Tlaloc, the computer center, the system, the anti-system, everything that moved and, of course, all that didn't move. I remember that, in the middle of my harsh remark, I also called Victoria a bastard, although this was nonsense to do at that moment. Once that bad word came out deep from my heart, loaded with lots of resentment, I felt like an invisible chain that I had around my neck, and that sometimes it was tight and suffocating me a little, had broken, and was leaving me free. Surprisingly, I felt better all the way around.

"Oh you fucking Victoria, you really had me screwed," I told myself relaxed and in a good mood, even though I knew that my shirt, socks, and shoes were sopping wet. Then—because I think about things with great logic—I added without losing my good mood and recognizing the fatality of my destiny, "Well, Javier, where there is an asshole, there is always an idiot. What can we do? Let's see if next time, you are a little more aware, and stop being the fool in the movie."

For some minutes, I was so absorbed in my catharsis and my thoughts that I forgot the annoyance of the rain. At that moment, I would have loved for my father, or someone very close, to hug me and tell me full of joy,

"Well done, boy, this is what you should do! You are getting rid of the poison that you had and it is now the time to get it all out. C'mon, I'll help you empty that stomach and clean out the bad blood in you."

I think that back then, I began to feel like someone important. They say that this often happens to the insignificant bureaucrats at some point in their work life. Anyway, I think that part of this was because my salary was not bad. With what I earned, I had enough to have lunch and dinner frequently in a very expensive restaurant. Sometimes, I hung out with my friends from university, and when one of them began to talk or brag about what he was earning, I realized that, at that time, I was the one who had the best income. Maybe this was what made me think that I had a promissory future at work. In addition, I also felt important because I could have been able to afford a trip to Paris, and all the ones I wanted to Cocoyoc, without affecting my finances.

If I had commented on these reflections to my parents, they wouldn't have guffawed, but they would have had a great smile on their faces full of tolerance, love, and wisdom that they couldn't have hidden too long. Besides, after having gone to the bathroom, or a bedroom, to laugh at me more discreetly for a while, they would have told me with great tenderness and all the patience in the world,

"Dear Javier, son, don't let yourself be deceived by appearances. There are other things that you should take into account; you must also not confuse the benefits of the moment with lasting personal achievements. We don't know if you know, but life is full of all types of illusions, and one must be cautious so as not to get trapped by one of these. These illusions are like black holes: you fall into one of them and you are screwed, because only until you die will you be freed from those hindrances, and only God knows what happened to your hopes and dreams of being someone. No, dear Javier, you must not believe anything from anyone, nor resign yourself to the plate they place in front of you. What if it is honey mixed with shit and it tastes good to you and you ask for more? No, no, son, you must always keep your eyes well opened."

When I reflected on this topic, I thought that my parents had made me feel like the grasshopper of the house, which had to be patient, open its eyes, and tomorrow try to be a little less foolish than it was yesterday. As to opening my eyes, I didn't have to do it toward the Sun, so that it would blind me, burn my retina, and make me walk haphazardly in semi-darkness for the rest of my life. Now, I had to set my mind on obtaining an attractive job that would benefit me lastingly. I realized that to achieve this, I couldn't spend my time coming and going from one building to another like a dumb bureaucrat or like a meowing bureaucrat, even though I had many personal achievements, which in reality, no one gave a damn about. For this reason, with great enthusiasm, I started to work on my Bachelor's degree thesis and then looked up for a university abroad that would accept me into the Master's course.

The idea of procuring a better future for myself motivated me for a long time and, fortunately, helped me distance myself from my sadness and emotional mishaps. I had, like the important politicians and famous businessmen say, to stop looking back and start looking forward. What happens is that, if I turn around, the *forward* that I had in front of me now corresponds to the *back* I had a while ago. So, without realizing it, one can get dizzy sooner than later along the way, if there was supposedly only one way that changes direction without notice. I think that, deep down, what was important was to do something new that, for better or worse, would lead me to reach a relevant achievement, something like a permanent change in professional and work status. Also, as the saying goes, don't look a gift horse in the mouth; so I imagined myself studying in a university abroad surrounded by beautiful Norwegian girls, and one or another French girl that would say something pretty in my ear. Frankly, I don't know how many cockroaches, bad information, or false expectations I had in my head at that time that the idea of going away to study sounded like anything but to be studying day and night, because the material one has to learn is enormous and the time to do it very short.

At that time, I realized that the problem that one has as a graduate student doesn't lie in the never-ending material one has to learn but in what people will say if one fails the Master's and in what will happen when one returns home. An enviable situation, given a pessimistic scenario, for me would have consisted in telling my parents:

"Hi, mommy and daddy, I'm back! I had an incredible time, and I spent all the money you gave me. How's that? Stop being so stunned and come welcome me, because I still love you, even though you didn't send me more money, huh? Oh, dear parents, come and hug me and tell me that you missed me, even though I never wrote to you or called you, and I only remembered you when the credit card you gave me began to be rejected at the bars and hovels. How mean you are! As you can see, I don't resent you much, and I'm sure that, over time, I will be able to forgive you. So, I'm back, but don't ask me to go and find a job because that's how aggressions start. Also, I would like to inform you that I'm exhausted. Can't you see me emaciated and with dark circles under my eyes? What do you think if to begin our relationship favorably, you start by advancing some money so I can go visit my friends, and you give me the keys to the most acceptable car that you have? C'mon, c'mon, I've told you, close your mouths and begin to cough up the money. Did you understand me?"

I wished that God would have granted that this situation in some way had applied to my person. Unfortunately, that was not my case, and my parents would have only walked me to the front door and would have told me,

"Son, you came in through this door. Well, through this door you will leave forever."

Passing or failing where I studied, I knew that I had to look forward and scratch myself with my nails because, just imagine, one leaves to study, and even though you spend your time studying like crazy all day and part of the night and weekends, pow! at the university, they come up with the affront that you have failed. If this had happened to me, I knew well that when I arrived home, my parents wouldn't tell me anything but would have only put the dunce's cap on me accompanied by loving pats on my back. I think that my mother and father, totally saddened and disappointed, would have told me,

"Oh, dear son, what will happen to you the day we die? We are going to be locked up in our coffins and worried that things will go bad for you in life. After all, as we see you and feel that you are a bit dumb for everything, we can't be at peace because we always have our hearts in our mouths. Dear son, don't take this wrong, but when we die, you can't count on us for anything, not even to tell you with much love what an idiot you are and a good-for-nothing. Oh, please take care of yourself and do things eagerly. Do you promise? Let's see if this way, you do better in the world than what we think; we are parents who worry their son won't be an eternal useless person."

These hypothetical conversations with my parents developed in my mind. In particular, the last one made me see my mother and father before their coffins were closed forever, with their faces disturbed from anguish and their hearts very distressed and crushed from the worry of thinking about how I would fare in my uncertain future. This scene that came to my mind was what motivated me to take very seriously my trip to study something that would not only serve me but also brace me up professionally. I did this and committed myself to making a great effort to not only look forward but always go forward in everything.

III
RAYMUNDO

"Come into my office," Raymundo said to me in a dry and sharp tone of voice from the door of his cubicle.

Something made me think, a moment before he called me, that Raymundo was carefully observing all my movements. I followed him. He didn't close the door and walked slowly to his desk. He went around it and pulled the chair back. He sat down with feigned calm. He never asked me to sit. Before starting the conversation, he put both his feet on the desk and looked at me, smiling. There, in front of me, was the real Raymundo, the one who had taken off his mask of false courtesy to show just who he was. According to what I had understood from the conversations of my fellow workers, Raymundo frequently harassed those at the office who depended on him, and while doing so, he felt happy.

"Javier, I wish to count on subordinates who are committed to the work and me. I expect that they do their job as I want; do you get it? From this moment, I want to put things clear: If you don't work, you leave. Don't worry, I'll take care of that. Is that clear?"

"Yes, Raymundo," I answered him, looking at him in the eyes, trying that the expression on my face didn't show any surprise or any feeling. Thinking about it thoroughly and with a certain retrospective, this scene had been expected. This is because of what my fellow workers had commented three months back when I joined the Studies Institute, Raymundo was a very difficult person who liked to play with people and, many times, he did it in a dirty way.

"I warn you, I will not tolerate any inefficiency. If you don't like the way I work, you have a problem that you know how to solve and what you have to do. I assure you, I'm not going to change; you are the subordinate, not me. That's how clear and transparent our work relationship is and will continue to be. I hope you will do things well, with no errors and exactly how I want them. As you know, since this morning, there has been a change in the functions and the organizational structure of the office. With these changes, I have become your immediate boss. I think that this was also made clear to you at the meeting this morning, right?"

I tried that my face did not show the disgust that Raymundo´s attitude and tone of voice produced in me. Indeed, as Raymundo said, there had been a change in the organizational structure of the office. I would stop depending on Jose Luis, one of the two sub-directors of the Institute, to now report to him, the other sub-director. As of this day, Raymundo and Jose Luis had interchanged activities. By the reception that I was being given at that moment, I thought that between Raymundo and Jose Luis, strong frictions were coming from way back. I think that my new boss thought that the adequate moment had come to begin to get even for past grievances. It is possible that, for having had a good relationship with my previous boss, I would be the object on which Raymundo could discharge part of the rancor that he had against Jose Luis. While bothering me, he indirectly attempted to do the same for my previous boss. If this didn't happen like that, then there was nothing to lament, because, for Raymundo, I was nobody, a waste of space, and at most, a subordinate that destiny had put at his disposition, without having to consult anyone. In the best of cases, I was a guy that he disliked and who, one way or another, he had to get rid of. If he had to be rude to me, then that was my problem and not his. I was the one who had all to lose; he just imposed discipline and demanded dedication and commitment from a subordinate. He would always present himself as the boss committed to the firm, and I would be the example of a bad employee, of the poor devil who doesn't understand what he is asked to do, nor does he know how to do it.

Raymundo waited a little to continue with his speech. He realized that I wouldn't let him see the displeasure that his words and, why not say it, his threats had produced in me. He had been my boss for not even an hour within the new organigram when he had already hastened to give me a sample of his way of being and how our work relationship was going to be. Maybe it was a mistake for me to have changed jobs a few months before. Although what had been my job position was still vacant in the financial entity where I had worked for over five years, I couldn't return to that place. When I gave notice of my resignation, I said that I was taking another job in which I expected to advance in my professional career. Rafael, my direct boss at the Development Bank, looked at me incredulously and annoyed when I told him that. He and I had already had a couple of confrontations, but since I did complete all the work that I was asked to do, Rafael didn't want me to abandon him. For my part, I was ill at ease in that office and, at some point, I had come to think that in the least expected moment, he and I could end up with blows.

"C'mon, Javier, no one progresses at work without being a team, and you've not wanted to do that with me. In addition, you are leaving for practically the same salary that you earn here," Rafael told me without hiding his discomfort. I didn't answer him. Deep down, I was not interested in dealing with him. I felt that he was a hypocrite who always wanted to be given explanations for everything that I did and for what the other companions said and thought. That already disgusted me. I remember very well the first meeting that the employees of the office had when he arrived as our boss in the financial entity. The work companions told me to applaud him. I didn't like that idea, and I asked them why they wanted me to do that.

"Do it for your good, you imbecile. Don't you know that this guy is famous for being a son of a bitch with the people? Applaud and smile. Don't you know that this has to be done in all jobs where a new boss arrives and there are rumors of cutting back on personnel?" the office mates said to me. They also told me not to ask silly questions. Besides, they had already asked here and there, and they had been told that the new boss, just like all others, liked to be flattered.

Later, it became clear to me that Rafael wanted all of us who worked for him as his "unconditional ones." On one of his birthdays, someone brought a mariachi and an organ grinder. The spectacle lasted a couple of hours. He felt, as the song says, like "The King" of the event. Certain people who worked in our area wanted him to feel like that. Then, the following day, the organizers of the feast for Rafael charged us all a proportional part of the cost of the party. I pulled out my wallet, and at that moment, I told myself, "Damn it. Whenever I can, I will leave this place of wheedlers, to get away from this type of people and bosses." Then, I opened my wallet to take out a couple of bills that I most wanted to throw on the floor as a sign of protest and contempt.

One of my work companions who was collecting the money for the event took notice of my annoyance and told me,

"I, the same as you, am irritated for having to pay from my pocket for a party for a shit-eater, but listen to me well, we have no option but to do it and wish that no one goes to the boss with the story that we put a long face or showed revulsion because if that guy finds out that we did that, he is capable of screwing us on the first occasion that he has."

"Ok. Ok. You're right," I said to him trying to hide my annoyance.

Who was going to tell me that Rafael was not such a bad boss compared to Raymundo? With time, I thought, full of irony, who knows if I would gain certain affection for that little squirt, who reminded me of some famous boxer of the past, or if I would have fought to death with him.

Besides, I had left the job that I had at the Development Bank because I wanted to do something more related to my career again, instead of guessing what my boss was thinking, so he would always be satisfied and happy. Now, I was realizing that that story had not changed. In the here and now where I was standing, I also had to be guessing what it was that Raymundo wanted to avoid that the ill will that he always had against me would become greater and get out of control, with worse consequences for me.

In perspective, I think that, possibly, if I had tried, Rafael would have received me again in my previous job, on one hand reluctantly, and on the other, happy that I was back to do the work. Rafael, the same as Raymundo, would also find a way to make me pay for the "blunder" and daring of having gone out to seek another job to try to advance professionally. Instead, there in front of my immediate presence, Raymundo was charging me for the "audacity" of having entered the same place where he worked before having consulted it or asked for his authorization. If he were hostile, who could reproach him? He only wanted to make it clear that he liked hard-working and dedicated people. Anything else could be interpreted as unsubstantial and senseless speculation, which could even be intended to discredit him in the office with an unfounded complaint regarding his way of being.

Raymundo, based on the authority that the Institute had delegated to him, did not commit work harassment toward me, which would never be possible; nevertheless, in a strict and very clear sense, he asked for efficiency from a new collaborator. There was nothing wrong in that or with anything related to it because, as anyone could say, those are the rules of the game in any job, in any subordinate job. Also, it was always better for the employee to know all the norms, the details, and everything that was expected of him because, in this constructive way, future problems were avoided. If this didn't happen, then nobody would find it strange that there would be problems, and that the one responsible was the inept employee who hadn't understood a substantial part of his responsibilities.

"Is everything understood, Javier? Do you have any questions? Is there something that you would like to talk over with me now? Do you feel sufficiently capable to work for me?"

Raymundo asked me these questions in a soft tone. He waited a few seconds and then smiled. He was making fun of me, and you could see from all sides that he was feeling happy. I was sure that he had prepared this scene in detail and had reviewed it in his mind several times to care about the impact that all his gestures and each of his words would have on me. I think that several days before, Jose Luis knew how the new structure of the office was going to be. On the other hand, Raymundo only had to wait for the adjustment of the personnel to be official to call me to his office and immediately bring me up-to-date details, with or without harshness, of how our future work relationship would be. His concerns and possible disagreements were placed on the table. Of what could I complain? I thought that from his perspective, I couldn't be, under any circumstance, upset, but instead, I should be, up to a certain point, grateful because without realizing it, he had been totally honest and transparent with me.

"Yes, Raymundo, everything is clear. Anything else you want to tell me?" I asked him, with serenity. My intention wasn't to make fun of him or to challenge him but to have an idea of up to what point he wanted to damage me, in addition to what he had already been explicit about. I also knew that this was the worst time to mock him or whoever was my boss. Any comment that I could make and that Raymundo didn't like, he could use as an excuse to bring it to bear against me later. In face of any question, he could easily tell the managers of the Institute,

"The thing is that Javier didn't want to collaborate from the beginning, as it had been expected from a person as prepared as he's supposed to be. I commented on this point with him a couple of times. You all can see that his work is not bad, but it is his attitude that leaves much to be desired, and that is what is affecting his performance. If someone doesn't wear the Institute's shirt from the first day, then what can be expected of him each day he comes to work? Besides, when I spoke with Javier, he was given the opportunity from the start, but it is clear that he didn't want to take advantage of it. His rebelliousness or mediocrity, I don't know how to call it, ended by imposing itself, and it is also true that the Institute cannot have the luxury of hiring this type of people if it wishes to preserve its profile of seriousness and professionalism that characterizes it."

Raymundo could have easily added these comments to show that he also had a positive side and that it was true that he had never thought of abusing his authority in relationships with his subordinates.

"Nothing. I have nothing more to say, Javier. I cannot be more transparent. You know it. You can leave for now. I need you to make a report. Later, I'll give you the details. Little by little, we'll get to know each other. In my case, I'll know which are your deficiencies and limitations, or, are you going to tell me that you don't have any?"

Raymundo asked me that question with sarcasm. He scrutinized my face at all times. He made me realize that we would play cat and mouse. I would be the inept and clumsy rodent, and he would be the audacious feline that uses its counterpart for entertainment. One day, the cat eliminates the mouse by mistake, because somebody has predisposed it that way, or maybe because it remembers that it has ancestral obligations to meet. Who could question the little feline if it was only doing its duty? Also, one mustn't forget that the cat always has to remind the inferior species that some were born to command and others to obey, as it also happens among bosses and subordinates, in any job and in all parts of the world.

"You can go," he said and stopped paying attention to me.

I thought that Raymundo had ended the meeting because, in the mental scheme that he had worked out about how the talk would develop, I could not have stayed listening to him impassively. He thought that he had already given me excess information when he made evident the threat, and then, he gave me the details of how he would exceed the limits of the warning. I left his office walking firmly, making him and the other office mates understand that the words and the warnings of who now was my boss had neither affected me nor intimidated me.

The secretaries and the other office mates heard everything that Raymundo had said to me, because he had intentionally left the door of his office open. I'm also sure that Jose Luis heard everything that Raymundo told me, because his cubicle is next to that of my new boss and the door of his little office was also open.

No one asked me directly how things went in Raymundo's office. From how my fellow workers looked at me since I left the office of my new boss until I got to my desk, I felt that they all wanted me to tell them how I felt about the reception that he had given me from the first moment in which we both started to work together.

At some point, I thought that if I was the mouse, then I didn't have to commit stupidities, or fall into the first trap in front of me. I had to make everybody in the office believe that Raymundo's words hadn't affected me. He had only informed me of the consequences that there would be from the errors that a collaborator that didn't make an effort to be efficient could commit. We can all have faults and limitations, but it was forbidden to have them if Raymundo were the boss. Only the spring water is clearer.

In time, I confirmed that my reaction had been the best. All office mates realized that for me, Raymundo's challenge was only a warning, perhaps hard and detailed, but that it had not intimidated me. My fellow workers were surprised. They were expecting me to become annoyed or indignant. Perhaps, some would have liked to see me leave the office of my new boss angrily, about to explode, and only waiting for the first opportunity to curse him in public and seek some solidarity from the maltreatment that I had received.

They all had seen that, while Raymundo had been talking to me, he had put his feet on the desk. We all had it clear that for my new boss, I didn't merit any consideration, but only offenses and humiliation. What could I expect from him? More similar situations and more humiliation? Surely, I would have more threats from him until one day, one of us would end the working relationship, he by firing me or, if I was lucky, me by resigning because I had gotten another job.

I remember walking calmly in front of all other fellow workers all the way to my desk. I felt that my rage was creeping up on me and was beginning to go through my whole body. I smiled at people on my way; perhaps my face was beginning to decompose. I thought that all my office mates were feeling sorry for me and were saying among themselves without opening their mouths,

"Look, there's Javier. Poor devil; frankly he's pitiful. Raymundo has upset him. Sooner or later, he's going to burst. He has already been through this humiliation, who knows how many more await him and with how much brutality Raymundo wants to irritate him. Ok, Raymundo is a great son of bitch; all of us at the office know that. What we see that is happening with Javier, we have to take as a lesson, since nobody gains by confronting Raymundo. The best thing to do is to not quarrel, to recognize that he is the boss, and that there is nothing to do about it. Also, we must not lose Javier from sight. Whatever happened to him could happen to any of us. We have nothing to do but to avoid playing cat and mouse with Raymundo, because he, as the cat or mouse, doesn't matter, will always cheat and will seek to screw up the other by any means necessary."

I got to my desk. Everyone was attentive to my movements. I sat in front of my computer. I opened the worksheet and took the mouse to begin to work. At that moment, the device I had in my hand was not the one that allowed me to get someplace on the screen; rather, it was an enormous steel pipe, which I held tight with force and full of hate and resentment. I felt that if I pressed the mouse that I had in my hand a little harder, it would break. At that moment, I realized that I had to calm down, and I repeated to myself in silence, paused, and with force,

"Raymundo, you're only a mangy son of a bitch. When you were born, your mother was disgusted." I repeated this phrase several times in my mind until, little by little, I was able to relax. I breathed deeply a couple of times, and then kept looking at the computer screen without thinking about anything. Later, without wanting to, my voice told me in silence,

"I'm the mouse with which you're going to have fun, Raymundo, and the one you will want to continue to humiliate every time you can or want. Here I am. I haven't gone, and I don't know when I'll be able to. I'm only telling you that I'm not hiding, nor will I hide. I promise that, on my part, I'll make a great effort to avoid any clumsiness."

These words didn't come out of my mouth. I breathed deeply once again. Without me wanting to, my mind continued to be active, with more ideas flowing and reflecting on my state of being.

"Raymundo, I am obedient, but I won't kneel, and much less before you. I only want to write in the air so that only you know that I wish your blood to rot and that you, like the mangy and revolting dog that you are, will soon howl from pain during the day and the night. I also want that rabies to blind you and make you chase your own shadow and tail without repose, so that you will mangle them full of hate and pleasure. Then, as the scum that you are, you will drop to sleep tired out and full of rage. When you wake up, you'll only drag yourself and the rats, one by one, will come and nail their filthy fangs in you so that you'll continue to be transformed into the repugnant and stinky garbage that is inside of you. At some point, someone will throw your decomposed body into trash. While they're doing that, they will feel the disgust invading their whole self, and they will be about to throw up. In a short while, they will throw up and they'll do it on top of what is left of you."

This mental vent relaxed me. It lasted a few minutes. Once again, I breathed deeply and continuously several times. When I stopped doing these inhalations, I felt that, in some way, I had helped myself to return to a certain emotional normality. I got to work as if nothing had happened, as if what I had lived that morning had been an unpleasant nightmare that never again would be repeated.

I left the office at the same time as always. On my way home, I remembered all the details of the meeting I had with Raymundo. I had his tone of voice in my mind, his mocking smile, all his words and, of course, at all times, I saw the sole of his shoes on his desk. I got home without realizing it. I tried to distract myself and avoid calling the attention of my wife and daughter.

"Is there something wrong, Javier? I see that you are tense. I don't know, but I think you're annoyed and you look a little decomposed," Lorena, my wife, told me, a little after I arrived home.

"It's nothing, Lorena. Don't worry," I answered her, trying for my voice to sound as normal as possible. I sought a novel and tried to take refuge by reading it.

"Is that so? Do you want anything for dinner? If you're hungry, I'll prepare something for you," my wife told me, perceiving that something was wrong.

At dinner time, Lorena asked me again if something was wrong. I think I couldn't continue to hide the uneasiness that the scene with Raymundo had caused me. I realized that my wife was already concerned about my attitude and that my daughter had not yet noticed my state of being. I didn't want to think about it, but I was certain that sooner or later, my boss would seek to get rid of me in a way that would hurt and humiliate me the most. That was beginning to cause me anguish, because I knew when that happened, I would have to go out and look for a job in an unfavorable situation or moment. Someone, maybe in an interview when seeking employment, would ask me,

"So, why didn't you adjust yourself to the style of your previous boss?"

How would I be able to respond to that person so that he would believe what had happened?

"I see you are very serious, Javier. I think something is worrying you very much," Lorena said to me.

By the tone of her voice, I noticed that she was uneasy and nervous. I tried to smile. Again, I told her that nothing was wrong with me. Maybe my tone of voice or the expression on my face was not convincing. I thought she was looking at me disconcerted and with a certain fear that something bad had happened to me. Without me realizing it, my daughter had come close to Lorena. The two of them observed me. I also noticed that my daughter was surprised. The two of them began to get anguished. I thought that anyone at seven years old is already conscious of many more things than one imagines. When seeing the anxiety that their looks reflected, my breathing became agitated. For a moment, I went mute, and it took me some time to react. I could only say,

"Please, don't ask me any more questions, ok? I can only tell you that I'm not feeling well right now and that today, at the office, I had a very unpleasant day full of a lot of tension."

At that moment, I felt great pain in my throat. It was as if it were tearing me up inside and out. Then, my windpipe began to shut down strongly, while it appeared to me that, far away, a salivating mangy dog, which had been lying in ambush for me from a long time behind a desk, had hurled at my neck with fury. That maddened and irascible animal was happy and howling full of joy. That mangy beast first growled with absolute hostility, and then opened its snout to show the whole world its bloody fangs.

IV
THE ASSOCIATION

I started to work at the Analysis and Administration Association as a project manager. The first boss that I had at that job was Enito, the director, who felt that he had been born by the gods, perhaps not by those from the Olympus but certainly by the gods from the Mexican plutocracy. He only picked a quarrel with me to set a clear and wide division line between him and me, which would help me not to meddle in what was none of my business. From then on, he let me do my work with no great problem because frankly, he wasn't interested in what I was doing. For him, I was something like a bundle that is left on the corner of a closet, so it's not in the way, or a tree that is on the sidewalk across the street and it is known that it must never change place. In reality, he was an individual with his professional project, defined and independent from the firm where he worked, from all his fellow workers, and from everything else that could exist. That is, what was important for Enito was Enito himself. Anything or anyone else was useless, and we could all go to hell, although in silence because I think that he didn't like disturbance or noise.

I'm sure that for Enito, within the widest working context that one can imagine, all other employees of the Association were a nuisance or just didn't exist. When he was nervous, he would twist his little mustache on the right side with his right hand, and he was always complaining because his wife, whom he said belonged to the high society, or that she came from a wealthy family (I don't remember what all he said), used to spend abundantly. And he, for his part, had to work with zeal to keep the family expenses balanced with the income. Deep down, Enito resigned to this family situation because he felt that it was the cost of having married someone with a great presence in the social structure and with deeply rooted habits of grand-scale consumption and spending.

"Damn it! No money is enough with this lifestyle," Enito would say, between lamentation and anger, every time he found out that his wife had bought this or that, or that the credit card balance had increased much more than he had foreseen for that month. Then, according to what he said one day, he got fed up with the office and resigned to start working as a consultant and, in that way, multiplied his income. I think that, in part, he acted this way because he thought he was the best professional in the world. Frankly, I don't think that he even was a middling good professional, but I think that the poor guy had developed the Narcissistic personality disorder in the profession, and he felt he was an expert on all relevant, structural, and well, cultural, environmental, and even digestive topics. For this reason, one could assure that Enito was an extremely arrogant person who knew it all (at least that is what he used to say), and he wasn't there to solve anyone's problems because he had to focus on solving his own.

I think that Enito only wanted to get rich by being in a renowned, legal, and extraordinarily well-paid activity. In my unauthorized opinion, I think that Enito better decided to leave the Association by his own will, before they kick him out of his office, because, a little before he parted, the members of the Administration Board had named a new president for the firm with whom he had had sad, strong, and persistent disagreements.

When Enito found out that Mr. X would be the next president of the Association, he blurted out in public,

"Goddammit, things are fucked now, here's where things get tricky and the bastards that will come along with the new president are going to want to screw me up by blaming on me everything that went wrong. They are not going to like anything that I'll do in my work. They're going to tell me that this is fine, but why hadn't I done that other, this last was what had been expected of me and not just any mediocre activity. Fuck, things will not just get tricky, but also there will be a lot of sons of a bitch who will want to screw me over."

I think that when Enito said all these compromising words, he was quite drunk or quite tense. It can be that he feared that the worst scenario for his professional career would be met and that he would undergo almost irreparable discredit. There was someone who stated at the office that Enito had said those ugly words, which directly and indirectly referred to and qualified the new president and other members of the board because, at that moment, he was very intoxicated with alcohol and even more resentful with life when he pronounced them. Maybe—one of the employees of the organization surmised—on that day, our director had to pay the credit card bills of his wife and was annoyed, frustrated, and a slave to the circumstances and the family debts. It was presumable and understandable for Enito to feel that the Sun no longer warmed him. If month after month, the poor man received bunches of statements of accounts that he had to pay without saying a word, in addition to the sad family history, this came together with the still sadder work history that he was living.

What is true is that on more than one occasion in the not-too-distant past, Enito and the new president had raised their voices strongly. People in the office had heard the door slamming, and the two of them had been very close to coming to shoves and blows. Then, the secret was rumored that they both hated each other. That had to be true, judging from the expression on Enito's face during a time: his smile had turned into a grimace, the grimace in the face of a soul in grief, and the expression of a soul in grief in a little bit of paranoia and depression. All of this made his laughter seem off-key and like prolonged sobs. If I had been in Enito's shoes, I wouldn't have felt anything but the end of a work cycle where everything was getting complicated. For Enito, and anyone else, it was better, people would say, that here he ran away than to lament that here he perished.

In my discredited opinion, what happened was that Enito and Mr. X called each other bastards, perhaps not in a loud voice, but they always disdained one another in silence, softly, as it is done with someone you no longer tolerate, and you wait for the first opportunity to have him pay for all the grievances or to see how that rival is rotting in life. Enito knew this really well, and he opted better to leave, supposedly with his head held high and the tail between his legs than to get into problems, which could get even more complicated. Thus, our director, when leaving the Association, avoided being humiliated at the sessions of the Administration Board and to be told in public that he was a big stupid man, that he was showing that his work wasn't more than disgusting trash, and that thanks to him, the firm had begun to have financial problems, that his trembling pulse was that of a habitual drunk, and that it would never be the firm and decided pulse of the captain of a company that can come through with flying colors from all types of challenges.

From afar, we remained watching the gossip, suppositions, and catastrophic predictions fair regarding what would happen to Enito first and then to the rest of us as employees of the organization. Everyone in the office, from the lowest to the highest positions, was nervous. We thought about the possibility that the new boss could reorganize the office, and so the doors of unemployment would open bitterly and for a long time for us.

Weeks went by and, just as we had expected, they named a new boss in Enito's place. This poor man didn't last too long at the Association. He wasn't liked by certain members of the Administration Board. His detractors said that he had to go because he was an appalling administrator. Those who supported him, which were the least, commented that he was watching the pesos and cents of the firm and that this was affecting the interests of some who stated that the money was there to strengthen the organization and that, therefore, it had to be spent generously in such and such a thing and in such and such a project. This new director surprised us. He treated all of us well and never sought any problems with anyone. He never used his position as chief to obtain personal benefits and special favors, nor did he want to bother his neighbor because there is nothing better to do. He was there almost a year, and then they changed him for an individual named Carlos, who, many years back, had been the director of the Association.

Some fellow workers said that Carlos, in his time, had left the firm running, breaking Olympic records. They then said that the accounting of the Association was a small or large disaster, that the accounts didn't match or couldn't be made to match, and that he resigned in a tacit gentleman's agreement so that no one would say anything and no one would review anything.

So, Carlos left and everything remained in suspense. Happily, and for many years, no one remembered Carlos at the office. Far, in someone's memory, there was the faded remembrance of Carlos as an overbearing chief or as an individual full of bad blood. But, since that had happened many years ago, people at the office didn't remember well the affronts and abuses that they had suffered, or rather, they didn't want to review that disagreeable passages from their past, where the current chief had been the protagonist. The parting of Carlos from the Association had been a breather and a hope for those who then worked there. Now, his return was a reason of concern for all employees.

They say, or rather that's how those who affirm they remember, full of authority, that one day, an old employee named Jorge arrived at the Association. He came to the office early and went to his cubicle. Time passed, and he was puzzled by so much serenity in the environment. It was strange to him that during the morning, he hadn't heard Carlos bawling out at some member of the office or insulting someone. He was famous for this because his words came out of his mouth generously, all wet with saliva, from the left side of his lips, and indicated greater animosity and hostility when they came out of the right side of his raucous chest.

"Listen, do you know if the chief is sick? I haven't heard him yelling nor have I seen him along the halls walking like a rabid dog," Jorge asked his fellow workers. They were incredulous that Jorge was so misinformed of the latest events at the office, and they laughed out loud and kindly told him,

"Don't you know that Carlos resigned yesterday and left running to the street, just with what he was wearing?"

"Praised be the Lord, and more praised be the audits," Jorge answered with such sincerity that the other employees looked in silence up to heaven as if, with that gesture, they wished to thank the Lord for the end of their work nightmares.

For many years, Carlos, at least in theory, had been like a test overcome for all those who then worked at the office. Years later, as if this was about the bitter turns of the fortune wheel called life, Carlos' friends, who now were followers of the new president of the organization, prepared for him a triumphal return to the Association.

Carlos arrived at the office one early Monday with great fanfare. That day, he sent for us all to be at a special meeting. Several times, he reminded us that he had already had the pleasure of having worked at the Association, and that, once again, he felt the great challenge of giving a total professional dedication as he had already done before. Obviously, everything that he would do would try to seek the strength and improvement of the firm. Then, he told us that our workplace was a great institution and that we should be proud to work in an entity such as that. Without me realizing it, most veteran employees began to applaud him. Someone who had just arrived would have thought that this reception was spontaneous and that it had a touch of nostalgia. I had already worked two years at the Association, and I didn't feel that was how things were, since people were smiling at the same time that their gazes were lost in the past, full of sadness, as if they had such an advanced cataract in their eyes that, in the next blinking, they would lose their sight forever and they all would be submerged in a dark, long, and dangerous tunnel from which they knew they would never be able to come out.

"Marta, why are they applauding? This seems like a pure and commonplace wheedling," I asked her in a low voice because she was standing next to me. I also asked her because while she now was Carlos' secretary, she had also been that of the previous directors, and my relationship with her had always been open and cordial. This background allowed me to trust her response. Besides, this scene reminded me of another one that I had experienced when I worked in another firm, and all fellow workers wanted to make a good impression on the chief.

"Javier, you just applaud. What's more, do it in such a way that Carlos will see that you are applauding him. Also, smile. I know what I'm telling you, and stop asking dumb questions that I can't answer and that no one who has worked here before would answer in their right mind," she told me in a low voice and always smiling.

Just like Marta, the other employees who had worked at the firm for many years began to shout several times with enthusiasm in a chorus, "Carlos! Carlos! Carlos!" to lift the new chief's morale. It all ended in spectacular cheers for our new director. Carlos' face was transformed. His gaze was lost in infinity, as if the presence of the old times had come to life with force before his eyes. For a prolonged moment, it seemed as if he was the happiest person in the world as if he held something in his hand that was called personal achievement and he already had it totally in his power. He remembered that once he stopped being the director of the Association, he wasn't anything again in the other organizations where he worked. This last labor situation has caused him tremendous pain and a great wound that perhaps never healed nor stopped hurting him, until this moment when he returned to the Association as its new director.

I began to applaud, and I felt like a big idiot or like a circus entertainer who had to go out running in the next thirty seconds to dress up quickly like a clown, and then does the same to show up as a bullet man, a buffoon, or whatever was necessary, or what the changing circumstances required. As I said, Carlos' face had been transformed. From every angle, he looked overwhelmed with happiness, because the reception that all employees had given him was beyond what he had expected. On his face, a great smile was outlined, and in his gaze, one could see the satisfaction of having achieved an important and almost unreachable work goal. Who was going to say it? In the past, it had seemed that, first, Carlos had left the firm forever on bad terms; but now, years later, it seemed that he had returned carried on someone's shoulders as the hero of the town, who had avoided a tremendous catastrophe and saved everyone.

"C'mon, of course, life is like a fortune wheel that today drags you and sadly rolls you somewhere, and then brings you joyfully back over here," I said to myself in a philosophical tone.

After applauding a while longer and seeing my fellow workers' attitude, I thought,

"Damn it, why do I think that this guy is an utterly lost self-centered person? He's going to ask all of us to make him offerings, kiss his hand, and that we enter his office only by dragging ourselves on the floor and not on the walls.

This smells like a very obstructed sewer pipe, and everyone here in the office seems to be very happy about standing on top of it and breathing the full lungs of the repulsive gases it ejects. This is nothing but smiling like an imbecile and in a completely pathetic way, while one is happily inhaling pure putrefaction. Oh, God! How difficult it is to work sometimes, and how miserable one is while working!"

In reality, the other employees of the organization were nervous and uncertain about their future in the firm. Some fellow workers asked themselves,

"Why did this idiot return to the firm? What does that despicable son of a bitch want from us? If he is so good for jobs, why didn't he go to another place with greater prestige than our squalid Association?"

"He returned to screw us, to charge for old debts," others answered with nervous smiles and in low, almost inaudible voices.

On that day, I got home and told my wife that we had a new boss at the office, and I gave her a brief description of the special meeting that we had. She listened attentively.

"We'll see how that guy behaves. God willing, he won't come to complicate the lives of all of us who work at the Association. He is causing me apprehension already, because those employees, who had been working at the office for many years, began to applaud him without an apparent reason, and he, like a fool, immediately had a facial expression of a happy politician. You should have seen how his gaze was transformed. It seemed like his smile surged from the deepest part of his being and his ambitions; in addition, he gave the impression that he had placed his gaze on the infinite," I told her a little worried.

"Javier, as long as that Carlos is not the same as the other bosses you have had in the past, things can be managed, don't you think?" Lorena asked me, trying to instill courage in me and so that I would think that my immediate work future wasn't going to be as dark as I thought. At that moment, I thought that I would know it—for better or for worse, anytime soon or whenever Carlos would feel comfortable, with no pressure. That is, once he became self-confident and on any day when he would be rushing, at some time soon, he would forget to wear his mask.

V

MY ASSISTANT

A few months after Carlos arrived at the Association, I was left without an assistant. No one asked me, but someone contracted Patty as my new collaborator. I gazed at her longingly from the first time I saw her. She was at least ten years younger to me, a white-skinned brunette and statuesque. I bet her measurements were 92-60-90. As it sometimes turned out, she had studied something which in today's work life doesn't guarantee a job, and someone had recommended her to somebody else, and just like that, as part of a chain of recommendations from friends and acquaintances, destiny brought her to the Association. I think that she didn't like the work, but she made her best effort to adapt and do things well. I—even though it might seem that I play the innocent—from the very start of our relationship, treated her well and never went too far as her boss asking her to do useless tasks or demanding her to do activities that would bring me personal benefit, as the large majority of bosses that I had before had done.

If Patty had been at least some three inches taller, maybe she would have been a famous model, who would frequently appear in women's magazines, promoting expensive clothes and sometimes letting see some part of her beautiful body in men's magazines. Undoubtedly, I think that those publications would assign her high-impact sections that are reserved for great maddening beauties who are pictured in photographs where they are wearing little clothes (maybe a pretty hat or some showy dress shoes) or nothing at all.

Patty's character was more agreeable than that of most models because the ones that I've known think that they have a porcelain face, silver bosoms, marble gluteus—because they are not wrinkled and will never be—a 24 or more carats gold vagina, and also that love exists as long as a there is a juicy checking account or some incredible vacations in a luxury yacht sailing slowly through the Adriatic Sea, while the tired Sun begins to set.

Little by little I became used to Patty's presence, although, I confess, that the day after her arrival, from very early, I wanted to go to the office to see her again. A few weeks later, rumbling in my mind were all her "Good morning, Sir, Good afternoon, Sir, Good evening, Sir," not knowing what they meant neither in my mood nor our work relationship. Honestly, I have to add that it was very nice to hear her and more agreeable to see her, even though I don't know how I would define "nice and agreeable," but just perhaps as something that made me sigh once and once again and to remember her paralyzing and beautiful figure.

As the weeks passed, she began to come in with more confidence about what my "office" was, what could be called an office without a door. Patty and I would talk a while about this and that and, if I remember well, about the lyrics of Jose Alfredo's songs. We would also devote ourselves to long reflections about the reasons why the songs by Juan Gabriel ("Juanga") were popular, and we wondered when Monsivais would write an essay in which he would compare Jose Alfredo with "Juanga" and would talk lucidly about their virtues, limitations, and similitudes.

On one occasion, Patty saw that I was calling some book stores to obtain a list of books that my daughter needed for her school.

"Sir, leave that to me. I'll take care of that, don't worry," she told me with a pretty and angelical smile. By the next day, Patty had already gotten all textbooks that my daughter needed.

"Patty, you don't know how grateful I am that you helped me to find my daughter's books," I told her with total honesty.

"Don't you worry, Sir, it was nothing," she answered with an even prettier and more angelical smile than the day before. I don't know why but, for a moment, I felt she hadn't smiled, but sent a tender kiss, like one of those with which

I dreamed about when I was a child and the daughters of my mother's friends, who were older than me and their bodies were already totally formed, hugged me tenderly and said pretty things to me, which made me melt from the inside.

One day, Patty told me that she liked cross-country and running on clay routes. She also commented that she loved to be in contact with nature. All of this made me think that she was a sportswoman by conviction and an environmentalist by devotion, as she, on one occasion, described herself.

"The thing is that yesterday I ran on the pavement, and look, Sir, I hurt my knee. Touch it, isn't it so that you can feel a small ball there in the middle?" she asked me. When I heard her words and saw her beautiful legs, I felt that the little ball that I have in the middle of my body would not take long to be altered. Then, I started to get a little nervous, and I stuttered when I spoke,

"Oh, Patty, how tremendous! You could have really hurt yourself. Did you hurt your other knee?" I asked her without taking my eyes off her legs. To make it easy for me to see her muscle injuries, she lifted the skirt to half of her dreamy thigh.

"Yes, but that was a long time ago. I think it's ok now. Touch it too, Sir, isn't it so that you can't feel anything?" she asked. As I extended my hand to touch that adorable part of her body, inside, I was beginning to feel everything, but mainly dizzy, the start of excitement, some lack of air, and high blood pressure.

"Yes, it's very smooth from top to bottom and also from the front to the back. It feels like it should be quite elastic inside," I told Patty, with my best smile and the intonation that the best sports doctor should have. She smiled at me. I think she was thankful for my authentic and disinterested concern that she had no problems with her knees. It took me some seconds to stop looking at her legs and start looking at her face. My eyes found a beautiful smile.

"Thank you, Sir. Is there anything I can do for you?" she asked me with the most angelical expression that I already knew of her, and I don't know why but it was beginning to make me feel happy.

"Nothing, Patty, rest up," I told her, just about releasing an unending chain of sighs and, in my mind, running out to embrace her. Without knowing it, I asked myself why life is so cruel, why one comes to have bad thoughts, why there are such beautiful and delicate women in the world like Patty, why I was so happy when I was with her, and why I felt like a big and unfortunate idiot when this marvelous woman wasn't with me. At that moment, I wished that Patty would take just two steps and have a terrible muscular contracture in the high part of her two thighs, like those I had when I was young and played tennis. My sane and apparent disinterested intent was to again make serious auscultation of that part of her body to provide her with physical assistance and psychological support, like I had done for her knees. Now, the emotional support would be for her little thighs, and the affective and loving part could be more detailed and complete and would involve other parts of our bodies. Thus, little by little, she and I would come to know ourselves and, therefore, we could work as a team in everything she wanted and order with her angelical face.

I don't know when it happened, but Patty began to get into my head seriously. The night of the day of her little hurt knees, I dreamed of her. In that dream, or at that moment when, according to Freud, the unconsciousness is freed and it plays us foul because it brings out all the filth and the fever we have inside, Patty and I were alone in my office. She was dictating to me. I, with certain clumsiness, was writing in a notebook whatever she was telling me. I kneeled in front of her and leaned the notebook on her knees. Then, happy, I would show her what I had written. They were sheets and sheets that said Little Knees and Little Thighs. She would compliment me for my excellent handwriting and kiss me on my forehead. I had nothing else to do but to embrace her around her waist and everything else from her body that my hands could reach in such a convenient yet uncomfortable position. Everything was going a good way for me until the damn alarm clock sounded, and I returned to my sad and monotonous reality where Patty, with all and her little knees and little thighs, was not present.

"Are you all right, Javier? Is there something wrong? You woke up very excited. You gave me the impression that you were quite nervous," my wife told me, standing in front of the bed. "It seems like a little while ago, you were dreaming about something that you liked because you didn't stop smiling. Well, get up now, you have to go to work."

"Yes, I do think that these last few weeks, I've been more nervous than normal and I need to sleep a little more," I answered her just to say something. Frankly, I didn't lie to her, since what I had told her was true. At that moment, I felt that Patty, just like the images of my dreams, had escaped through some hidden door that was more out of my sight than from my subconsciousness. Before I got up, I remembered that I would see her in a little while. I went to take a bath, and I don't remember if it was intentional, but I took it with cold water.

"Just like that, Javier, only with iced water baths is that fever going to leave you and you are going to be able to behave at the office," I said to myself while the iced liquid fell on top of my body. I recognize that my thoughts combined some sadness with a lot of frustration. I sighed and thought that I didn't know what I would have done at that moment if Patty and I had been alone and naked at the office.

One summer day, when it was really hot, Patty arrived at the office in a miniskirt. I think that from the place where someone was situated, you could see her tonsils and other things of her showy and pretty body. Damn it, that day I couldn't concentrate on my activities, and Carlos, the boss, kept asking for things. First, he had requested a report, then a series of graphs, and finally, a presentation of some nonsense, not related to the activities of the Association, but despite everything, I had to turn in to him all the reports he requested. That day, as on many others before, Carlos was in a bad mood, and he had already shouted at half of the personnel of the office. Because of the way the director was behaving, I felt uncomfortable and pressured. In addition, I was suffering in another way each time I saw Patty. I could not concentrate totally on my work. I made a great effort and finished everything Carlos had requested. I ended the work a little before lunchtime. I told Patty to take advantage of the fact that we had sent the material that had been requested of us and for her to go eat. I saw that she picked up her things, and before she left, she came to tell me,

"Sir, have a good lunch."

I smiled at Patty and felt happy. Also, I saw how her beautiful legs transported the rest of her shocking body. I think that at that moment, I sighed like a million times in less than a second.

Before going home to eat, I also kept thinking about Patty and what I felt toward women like that, in general, as if they were something that I could go without for a long time, at least theoretically. I breathed deeply and imagined that I was walking on the beaches of Puerto Vallarta, and that, next to me, a sculptured American woman in a tiny bikini, more beautiful than any Miss Universe, was taking the sun. That is, I lied to myself a little, and I didn't think about Patty directly or immediately. Well, in my dreamy state, I thought that to begin to chat with the hypothetical beautiful American woman, who for some profound psychological and strange reason, looked a lot like Patty, I should say to her, *Hey sweetie, I think I have seen those beautiful eyes before in…* and then I would refer to a city. I kept thinking.

"Maybe Paris, Venice, or Amsterdam could work," I told myself with total conviction, although at that moment, I knew that I had never been to Amsterdam. "I could also include San Miguel de Allende," I thought to incorporate to that list of cities one from Mexico.

The point here was that for the strategy of communication to be successful, I would have to tell her—the American girl or Patty—that her eyes were very pretty. If I told either of those two sculptural women that they had pretty legs, perfect buttocks, and that their breasts were prettier than any I had ever seen in my life, then those ladies would not hesitate to guess that I was only thinking about having sex with them, and not in any other loving or tender thing that could interest them. However, if I told them that I liked their eyes, then they could think that my interest in their person was genuine, disinterested, and more spiritual than sensual because, in the measure in which the eyes are the mirror of the soul (that is what is said), those beautiful women would consider that I was only interested in that their souls would know mine, maybe to save it and to keep it on the right track.

"Of course, for all these things to happen, our bodies must know each other completely and with intensity," I reasoned happily. Then, full of conviction, I closed my eyes and with all the mental power that I had, I told her in silence,

"Oh, Patty, what beautiful eyes you have!"

At the time, when my mind articulated that phrase, I considered the possibility of saying it out loud because I was sure that no one was listening to me. I thought that my telepathic message would reach Patty while she was having her lunch and that she would sweetly remember me at dessert time.

That afternoon, I went to have lunch at home and returned to the office hurriedly. Throughout the rest of the day, I realized that I had important and indisputable psychic powers. Around six in the afternoon, Patty came into my office, very smiley. She asked me how I was. Then, she came close to me and leaned on my desk. With one hand, she pushed some books aside and lifted her right leg. The left one was anchored to the floor, and she twisted her body towards me. Oh, God! I'm glad that at that time, women used panties and not tiny thongs! I would have fainted right there, or I would have had an asthma attack. I felt my blood pressure rising uncontrollably like surging waves, and the emotion was suffocating me. I had become mute, my retina had dilated, I had a face of an idiot, my body didn't want to obey me and, of course, my whole self was rigid and paralyzed.

"Patty, what do you know about Paris?" I don't know why I asked her that trivial and dumb question. Maybe I did it to break the asphyxiating ice that I felt inside me, although I knew well it wasn't ice, because it felt like fire, or maybe I did it just to see what turn the conversation and my emotions would take.

"Oh, Sir, a little, not much, but I would fall in love in Paris, Venice, Amsterdam, or even in San Miguel de Allende. All of these are the cities of my dreams. And you, Sir, where would you fall in love? Don't tell me, because I imagine that with those pretty eyes that you have, any woman would fall madly in love with you," she told me with the greatest tenderness possible, and she put her right hand on one of mine. I felt that, from the waist up, I was beginning to tremble and, from the waist down, it had been a while that I was trembling.

When she held my hand between hers, she leaned forward. Her blouse, by a blessed coincidence, was plenty unbuttoned. I almost breathed close to her breasts. They smelled of roses and other showy and splendid flowers in the field. Due to technical reasons, I couldn't see her breasts totally (the damn mini bra that she was wearing impeded me from doing it), but since I had my eyes well opened, they were full of joy with the marvelous and stimulating 95 percent that I was able to see of each one of her gorgeous and soft breasts. Inside, I was juggling emotionally to avoid my hands from disobeying me and directed to touching those stimulating, captivating, and, I imagined, soft parts of Patty's body.

"Oh, Patty, Patty, Patty, oh Patty! Well, don't say those things, right? I think that all of us would like to fall in love in those cities or, at least, to walk through their streets with our loved ones, don't you think so?"

"Oh, Sir, it seems to me like you can foretell my thoughts. The idea also came to my mind of walking through the streets of those cities in the company of my loved one. Imagine, what an incredible emotion it would be to kiss the loved one, having as a background the Eiffel Tower or the pretty and peaceful cobblestone streets of San Miguel. What beautiful thoughts you have, Sir!" Patty told me, happy and excited.

I listened to Patty's words and blushed. Without my intention, she embraced me, and at that moment, my nose and the rest of my face were slightly in contact with her gorgeous and indescribable breasts. That embrace electrified my whole body. The effect was particularly more intense in the waist down area than in the rest of my body. Oh, God! In silence, I told myself and almost implored silently, *Patty, Patty, Patty, by divine charity allow me to squash everything that I can squash of your beautiful body and I promise you that you and I will be eternally happy.*

"Changing the subject, Patty, what do you think about the job?" I asked her, not knowing what to tell her and not knowing what to ask her, and not sure if I was breathing, dreaming, delirious, or if I was talking to the wall where someone had drawn a woman identical to her. At that moment, I felt that she, Patty, had cast a spell on me, hypnotized me, or put powerful magic powders in my food, or my drinks, or in the air that I was breathing, to have me stupid at her feet. Damn, I wanted someone to assure me that, at that moment, I was awake and everything that had happened, and that I had listened, seen, and softly smashed and caressed with my face, did happen.

"Well, Sir, I'll leave you, because, in a little while, I'll have to go. Today, for the first time since I've been working here with you, my boyfriend will be coming by to pick me up, and I have to hurry to be ready. If I take a long time to go down, Jorge, my boyfriend, goes crazy and sometimes tells me bad things. I've told him that he needs to calm down, but he doesn't pay any attention to me. I'm leaving. I send you a kiss," she said to me.

Patty walked some steps toward the exit of my office. Then, she made a half turn and put her right hand below her chin and extended it. There she placed a kiss and blew softly, I think with a lot of love, in my direction. Before turning around to leave my cubicle, she sent me a tender smile. I, on my part, began to suffocate.

The moment I knew that Patty had a boyfriend, I immediately began to feel, first, slight dizziness, and then, that the floor started to open below my feet. I felt that I was falling into a torrent of water that was dragging me away with force and at great speed and made my body and my self-esteem strike with force against enormous rocks. I tried to swim, but fast, I began to drown in the deepest and most plentiful part, I think, of the Amazon. At the same time, I had the composure of seeing how thousands of damned murderous piranhas were coming toward me to devour and finish my saddened and miserable person. I thought that this, my only body, didn't have salvation and would end up in smithereens at the bottom of the sea and that only the waves would take from here and there, without rhyme or reason, whatever was left of my torn garments and sad feelings.

I felt that and other horrible things the moment Patty told me that there was someone, for me, damned and loathsome, who already had a place in her heart. However, inside of me, I felt certain joy that illuminated me at that terrible and disconsolate moment: the damned piranhas and the detestable boyfriend could put an end to my body and my flesh, but the kiss that the most beautiful woman in the world had sent me moments before withdrawing from my office had remained treasured forever deep in my heart.

"No one can tear the kiss away that Patty sent me," I told myself as a matter of consolation, and with almost tears in my eyes, at the same time, I felt my body was light and began to float with each involuntary sigh that came out of my respiratory system.

I waited around five minutes sitting in my office. I don't know whether during that lapse I bit or chewed the nails of my two hands. Once I heard Patty going down the stairs (my cubicle was on the first floor of a house conditioned as an office), I went close to the window that faced the street. I saw that Patty was out on the street. Her steps were short and, to me, absolutely enchanting. The twerp of her boyfriend didn't open the door of the car for her. She got into the vehicle quickly.

"That good-for-nothing boyfriend of hers is nothing more than a bum who doesn't deserve Patty," I told myself fully convinced and annoyed. I also felt an acute and heart-rending pain that appeared in the upper left part of my chest.

From above, I observed how Patty's little thighs and dreamy little knees were settled into a comfortable position in the front seat of the car, thanks to her miniskirt. I felt as if someone had taken me to Paris to walk down the Champs Elysees to look through the show windows at the exquisite food that is served at those luxurious restaurants in that area. When I saw Patty from waist up, I thought of a delicious dish of tender double breast of chicken just baked; when my eyes stared at her lower extremities, I imagined some tasty mutton legs marinated in their juice, and when my sight was centered on the middle part of her body, I first thought about a very juicy cut of soft meat that is eaten with the fingers, and then, on some exquisite and fresh mussels.

Patty saw me from inside the car, and once again, she sent me a kiss. My poor and maddened eyes saw how this, like a speedy arrow sent by Cupid, passed through the windshield of the car, went uploaded with all the positive and prettiest sentiments existing on Earth and in the rest of the universe, and then, once passing through the window glass in silence, it rested sweetly in the middle of my heart. Oh, God! In that never-ending moment of love, I realized I was at the point of losing my sanity, that the world is a marvelous place to live in, and that it was urgent to be the next day in the morning to see Patty again and enjoy her company while I thoroughly caress with my sight each little piece of her gorgeous body.

That day, I got home and not realizing it, I took a long appeasing and necessary cold shower, twice. That kind of bath became part of my routine. Thanks to them, I could once again breathe normally every time I saw or was close to Patty. I also think that they helped me avoid, on more than one occasion, that I fainted before her most beautiful and delicate feet. If this home remedy had not calmed down the passion I felt for Patty, then I think I wouldn't have had any other alternative but to voluntarily enter a psychiatric hospital so that someone would listen to me and cure my ills.

"Give me Patty or give me electroshocks!" I would've implored the doctors on my knees, screaming, driven insane by love, once and once again from the infirmary.

"Poor me, my head is full of testosterone, and I don't have one sole neuron alive to reason," I told myself, I don't know at what moment full of sadness before going to sleep. "Oh. God! Why are women cruel?" I asked myself before sinking in the obscure unconsciousness that each one of us has and that frequently makes little absurd short movies in black and white regarding our sorrows, frustrations, and yearnings.

"Oh. God! Why have women who are beautiful to me also been cruel with my distressed, inoffensive, and charming person?" I asked myself in general, so as not to commit myself to a response in particular about Patty. I couldn't sleep easily. I analyzed my situation thoroughly. Thanks to a strong dose of frankness and to what life has shown me, I prescribed much Patty (all that I wanted) and more cold water baths (all that I needed). In the end, I fell asleep thinking about Patty.

The next day, a new routine began at the office. Patty would come to my place several times. She would sit on my desk as she usually did, one little leg here and the other over there. While she talked to me with her angelical voice, one day I began to take notes on my agenda: Monday, red; Tuesday white; Wednesday pink; and that's how I continued with the rest of the days of the week, the month, and the year. One afternoon, after lunch, I don't know what happened, but my agenda remained open, perhaps due to unforgivable negligence, on top of my desk. I think that I left it open where I had made my notes each time that Patty came to see me. She asked me something, and, luckily, or because that's what destiny had for me, I don't know, she saw what I had written.

"Oh Sir, what pretty handwriting you have! And, what is this?" she asked me looking at my eyes. I think what she saw that was written, awakened great curiosity in her, or, better said, a naughty curiosity. Her eyes brightened up and, for a fraction of a second, I saw that a beautiful smile was outlined on her face, which quickly vanished because she wanted to put a face that was of a serious and understanding person.

"I don't know, Patty. I think it's nonsense. Don't pay any attention to that. Sometimes, when I'm distracted or nervous, I write down things, without rhyme or reason, and then I don't remember what they were about. See? That's how half-crazy people are, don't you think?" I asked her, pretending to be as casual as possible. Then, I tried to change the conversation.

At that moment, I proposed to behave naturally, but stupidly and involuntarily I blushed. Before I began to curse my unconsciousness, I realized that Patty had noticed that I had blushed. She placed one of her delicate hands on mine. She looked at me full of sweetness and didn't say anything. At that instant, it seemed to me as if when the angels and the celestial world make us a gift of tenderness and affection and no one says anything, only the moment is lived intensely, which seems like an eternity, and the greatest gift that we receive in life is a look or a smile like those Patty was giving me at that moment. Also, in that sublime situation, our heart beats quickly, and we become sweeter and tastier than a just-baked sugar bun, like those our grandma prepared for us when we were kids, and everything was happiness and dreams for us.

The incident on my agenda passed as if nothing had happened. Now, Patty, instead of going to my place two or three times a day, as she had done in the past, went four or five times. At all times, she would smile at me. Several months went by in which she and I worked hard and efficiently, and I can affirm that we were immensely happy. Carlos never bothered us or called our attention, because we did everything that he wanted in time and form. Many weeks went by, and I don't know how many months in which I would dare to say, putting my hands in the fire, that being in the office had me full of joy and bliss. What else could I ask of life?

"Sir, I have a surprise for you. I'm sure you are going to like it very much. And, if you don't, you'll tell me the truth, right?" Patty told me on my birthday from the moment she arrived at the office. We began to work as usual. I was hoping that she would come to my desk at eleven in the morning but she didn't. Instead, I saw her passing by in the corridor. I imagined that she was pleased. She smiled at me and sent me one of those kisses that I was treasuring and numbering one after another in my afflicted heart. I saw that she went to the bathroom. She didn't take long to come out and came directly to my place. She looked pleased from all sides.

She began to talk with me and she sat, as usual, on my desk. It always took me about 15 seconds to look down, since someone who isn't a gentleman would have done it immediately, and that was not my case. I looked down. I couldn't believe my eyes. I was stupefied. I looked at her in the eyes, and I looked down again, and then I looked in her eyes one more time. First, I got nervous, and then I felt that my throat was closing from emotion and that enormous rivers of fire or lava were invading the middle part of my body. Patty was observing me. I think that she was having fun and was happy, and I, I confess, had the greatest erection in the world.

"Patty, love, queen, little princess, that's super, Oh! Don't you see that one day I'm going to be left without speech? These impressions are going to make me diabetic, or they are going to cause me multiple thromboses in my whole body or one of my veins is going to burst in some part of my frail and rickety brain. Oh, little queen, I think I can't any longer, and if I lose my speech forever, you're going to be responsible. Look, can't you see how I feel? I'm trembling from top to bottom and from bottom to top. I have to breathe deeply because I feel that I'm at the point of fainting and I don't know how long it will take me to recover my consciousness," I said to her with just a thin thread of afflicted voice, of the one that people say comes from beyond the grave, and with a look of authentic pain. It was an ache that came from my body's center of gravity, that is, my penis, to the center of gravity of my soul, that is, my penis. I felt that my soul was the most erotic thing that existed in the universe and its surroundings and that that intangible thing, which is the spirit, the essence, or whatever, had materialized in the most affectionate penis of the cosmic space of the Milky Way, whose only owner was Patty. Oh, God! At that moment, I felt illuminated from the flesh and that my life had only one mission, and it was called Patty.

"Sir, today is Friday and I also know that it is your birthday. I didn't know what gift to give you. Did you like it?" She asked me waiting for an answer. My face indicated happiness, and stupefaction and I don't know how many other emotions and other things. Instinctively, I embraced her as I had seen myself doing it in the dream where I wrote pages and pages of Little Knees and Little Thighs.

"Sir, this gift is only to be seen and not to be touched. When you recover, we'll put today's date on your agenda, and we'll write, 'Friday, January 5th. Nothing', just so we don't forget this beautiful day," Patty told me in my ear in the softest and most loving tone than can exist. I was only able to react by pressing my arms around her marvelous body so that she would feel that I had understood what she had told me.

When I was embracing Patty, I thought that as soon as I got home, the first thing I would do would be to remove a light bulb from a lamp in the living room that was connected to the power. Then, I would put in my index finger, for at least five minutes or until my internal equilibrium, my aura, and my chakras would stop sending insane flying sparks of emotion and light of all colors here and there, and my emotional chaos would relax. Also, I considered myself a fortunate person, because if my pupils were made of crystal, I told myself, they would have broken into a thousand pieces because of the beautiful and indescribable spectacle that they had witnessed thanks to Patty.

I arrived home. I was exhausted and my head hurt a lot. I greeted everyone with a kiss, even my daughter's boyfriend. I was happy. I loved the little dog that my wife had bought a couple of years ago, and which, even now, growls at me and attacks me with rage. A noble and deep sentiment that was in total effervescence inside me made me caress the head of that aggressive and many times ungrateful dog. That insensible animal didn't understand the sublime spiritual exaltation in which I was and growled at me several times. That damned animal, as always, mistrusted me. I didn't pay much attention to it, but I think it didn't attack me because the dog thought I was quite drunk. I didn't either argue with my wife. To my daughter, who was just seventeen, I gave all the permits that she wanted to have at her disposal in the coming twelve months. At first, my wife didn't give any credit to my words, but then she protested. I think she thought that when I was coming from the office, I had fallen into a deep ditch in the subway that was under construction, and that I had irreparably damaged my brain.

"Lorena, I feel sorry for our daughter, she has to start living, and what's better for her than to do it with the support of her loving parents," I told her in a soft and friendly voice, although I didn't see either my daughter or my wife, because both their faces were transformed into the face of a friendly and agreeable Patty.

"Mom, what's happening to my father? He must have hit his head or something like that, which hurt his brain. I think the poor man is now an idiot forever," my daughter said, terribly worried. I think a couple of tears slipped down her face and her voice was beginning to break.

I heard her, and my only wise response was to smile at them all. I went to the TV room. Without anyone seeing me, I took off the light bulb from a lamp. I licked well the right index and ring fingers. I sighed. I don't know if I did this just once or many times. Something that was coming from deep inside me was telling me with total conviction, strength, and love,

"Give me Patty or give me electroshocks."

I don't remember what happened after I had self-medicated myself with a dose of electric shock on my distressed body, to re-establish the equilibrium of my aura and the balance of my chakras. My wife then commented that the electric flow of the house had gone. She thought that the damned power company had played the usual dirty tricks by sending an overcharge to end with the Mexican middle class and their household appliances. So, after that surprise and consternation about what could have happened to the refrigerator, washing machine, and TV, due to the electric discharge, they found me thrown on the sofa.

"What happened, father? What were you doing with the lamp that you had in your hand?" my daughter asked me quite concerned and just about having many tears rolling down her eyes. I think at one moment she thought, with no reason at all, that I was going to commit suicide or that I had had an attack of insanity.

"How reckless you are, Javier, you almost killed your daughter and me from fright. But, what were you doing, there like an idiot, with the lamp?" my wife asked me full of curiosity. I already knew the tone of her voice. This one indicated to me that, suddenly, without any apparent motive, she could go from the most serious rebuke to embracing me and telling me most sweetly and lovingly,

"My poor little fool, didn't your parents, or anyone at school, ever tell you that you can't play with the electric current? Understood, my little fool?"

"Oh, I'm so dumb," I said, "I thought that the lamp was broken. I don't know what I did, that I just opened my eyes and I was on the floor next to the sofa," I said so to fake total dementia. Frankly, what else could I say? That I was thinking that my life was going to come to its senses in the coming future, only if it had constant sessions of electroshocks? Oh, I thought about it a little, and then I believed that it would be more convenient and believable if I just made a face of a fool. Given my complex emotional situation at the moment, I had no trouble putting on that face and generating certain constructive compassion toward my person from those surrounding me.

After the incident, I went to take a long and comforting bath with iced water. Liters and liters of cold water fell on my head and I never stopped seeing Patty. Once I calmed down a little and thought that Patty had already authorized me, I went to sleep.

"I need a little bit of inside peace and calm," I told my wife when she saw that I was putting on my pajamas.

"Yes, Javier, I think you need that, and perhaps something more. Just take it easy, ok? Nothing about getting up asleep at dawn and wanting to do little things, and when I say no, I mean no. Then you stay quiet for a while, almost without breathing, and then you fall into a deep sleep from which no one can get you out."

"Stories, Lorena, you are inventing stories."

"No, they aren't stories or fantasies, Javier, you've been like that for about three months and, now, it turns out that you didn't know and that you were only profoundly asleep and dreaming about I don't know what. Yeah right, and pigs can fly. Another thing, if you hadn't been so dumb with the light, we would have gone out to dinner to celebrate your birthday. Instead, just look, the only thing you gained with your craziness of wanting to pretend you are the failed electrician was to scare all of us," my wife told me with an ambivalent tone of voice that she sometimes used to stop a conversation or to lengthen it, as a preamble of a reprimand, or simply to make lighter and more bearable the existential pressure that she had deep inside her heart and on her fragile shoulders.

"A kiss, my Tom Thumb of two meters. The failed electrician of this house is tired and has to sleep," I told her and tried to disconnect myself from this world. I closed my eyes. Not much time went by when Patty came to me, dressed as a nurse. She entered the room quickly. She was wearing a very little mini skirt. In her right hand, she was carrying a small first-aid kit, and she smiled the moment she saw me.

"Where does it hurt, Sir? I've brought special medicine that I prepared for you and, if we have the time, I can even give you a massage where you think you most need it. Do you agree? Tell me where we can start to cure you. You can't just stay there feeling bad and all sick. I must cure all your ills, Sir."

"Patty, please, don't bother. Nothing happened to me. Besides, you know why I did it, right?"

"Oh Sir, I won't go away until I leave you as new. Where does it hurt? Where do I start?"

"Here, here, and here," I told her, pointing out first my penis, then my heart, and lastly my penis again.

"But, Sir, remember that I told you that the things that I showed you were only to be seen and not be touched. And the first thing that you do is to run out and touch the electric current. I think that you are a very disobedient boy. Let's see, repeat after me five consecutive times as follows:

"What Patty showed me is only to be seen and not to be touched."

"Patty you are asking me impossible things," I told her in a tone of voice full of pain and that, without meaning to, reflected all the weaknesses of my mind and my body.

"No, Javier, they are not impossible," a well-known strong voice that came from behind where Patty was standing told me. She heard those words. First, she was surprised, and then she was fearful, and at the least expected moment, she ran out. I stayed waiting for someone to appear. I was attentive for a long time and no one came.

Saturday and Sunday went by and I was exhausted and with a terrible headache. I said at home that the incident with the lamp had affected me, which was true to a great extent. I felt a lot of laziness, but at all times, I continued to see Patty's face. I think that the combination of the domestic electroshock with the cold water baths helped me not to go crazy, to calm down, and to make the weekend tolerable. I imagine the balance of my aura and my chakras was re-established in those days, or at least, it began to be.

I think I dreamed about Patty only on Saturday. I saw myself packing a huge suitcase, which I placed in the car. Then, I was driving the car and went to pick her up at her house. For a moment, I thought in my dream that she was the one who came to pick me up, but then the dream continued to flow normally, and at some moment, I saw myself getting out of the car and walking toward the door of her house. I didn't wait for her to open the door. With my right hand, I turned the handle, and then pushed the door open. She was waiting for me. When she saw me, she immediately jumped to my neck, as it always happens in good movies full of melodrama. Without noticing, she and I began to kiss each other like two adolescents who for the first time were knowing real physical love.

"Easy, sweetheart, easy, the love of your life has come for you," I told her with the utmost self-control in the world. "You and I are going to flee. The world is ours and we have to live it intensely. First, let's go to Acapulco, and then, we'll hide on Coronados Island or in San Javier, there in Baja California Sur, whatever you choose. Our only work and purpose will be to be happy for life," I told her, while I saw her face filled with total happiness before she began to give me another never-ending series of incredible and exciting kisses.

Sunday was a more restful day. I remember that I dreamt about Patty again. She and I were holding hands bathing naked in Nopolo Bay. We had gotten up early and had gone out to walk on the beach to see the dawn. The first sunrays lit up Patty's face and she said to me in silence,

"Sir, you don't know how much I love you!"

I was happy. Patty and I embraced, while the waves rocked our bodies tenderly, and our love was as great as the Sea of Cortes, and the whales of the whole world had met around us to attest that we were happier than Romeo and Juliet.

On Monday, as on any other working day, I went to the office. Frankly, the cold water bath I took that morning hadn't been sufficiently powerful to contain the flammable material that I had inside my person. This made me arrive at the office with a certain nervousness. The whole time, I waited to see Patty. A half-hour passed and she didn't arrive. I waited another while, and when I saw that she didn't arrive, I went down to Martha's office. I had the impression that those two were friends.

"Hi, Martha," I greeted her, "do you know whether Patty will be coming to work today?"

"Javier, I'm glad you've come to my office. You better sit down. Look, on Friday afternoon, almost when I was about to leave, Patty gave me this letter for you. She asked me to give it to you personally. Here you are," she told me.

Martha pulled out an envelope that was in a drawer of her desk. She gave it to me and then got up to leave me alone. I felt confounded and the scene had taken me by surprise. I thought that Patty was going to tell me in the letter that she was going to have a child of mine. With my heart beating fast in my chest and my temples, I discarded that possibility, because our bodies had unfortunately never come together for that to happen. I was extremely nervous. I thought that the worst was awaiting me. Patty was saying,

"Dear Sir,

"Today, as I told you earlier, is your birthday and it is also the last day that I will be working in the Association because I'm going to get married to Jorge, my boyfriend, this weekend. It's been a long time since I had made that decision, but working with you had complicated everything. On one occasion, I was at the point

of telling you that you are a robust man and that we women like that type of man, but then I thought that you would think that I only wanted to go to bed with you and not establish a lasting loving relationship between us. On another occasion, I thought about telling you that you have beautiful eyes because I confess that I do believe that the eyes are the mirror of the soul, in addition to that I always liked your eyes very much.

"Sir, if you knew how hard it's been to separate myself from you. When I arrived at the Association, I thought that I wasn't going to last very long in what at that time was my new job. See, we worked together for almost two years. In those months, time went flying for me, and I can swear that that epoch has been one of the happiest of my life. I would wake up early in the mornings, because I wanted to get to the office to be able to see you and talk to you about this and that, and about all those topics that entertained us. I think that the spontaneous way in which we always communicated with each other always made me see with affection your person, and this affection grew and grew inside of me in an unstoppable way. I did dumb things, not just to call your attention but so that you felt well and more relaxed. Sometimes, I perceived that you were tense when the work accumulated and we had little time to do it. On one of those occasions, it occurred to me to do things that would help you relax and see that the office routine is different. I don't regret any of the dumb things that I did, because I never hurt anyone, and they served for you to see the office activities with other eyes and with greater enthusiasm.

"Sir, I also would like to tell you that you have no idea how much I enjoyed our talks on 'Macario', 'Hegel and me', 'Roots, A Mexican Town that Walks', the songs of Jose Alfredo, and Juan Gabriel and everything else. Then, when work had to be done, we always did it with dedication, and at all times, I felt that we made a good team, in addition to that you were always very patient with me and you taught me many technical things that without your help I would have never understood."

"After the office, I used to go home, and on various occasions, I dreamed about you, and we both lived very agreeable moments full of happiness. A few weeks ago, I had a dream in which you came by to pick me up at the apartment

where I live. First, we both were going to Acapulco very happy, and then to incredible and little-known places of Baja California Sur. In some dreamy place of that state, you and I would get into the sea, and then I felt our relationship was as big as the whole Sea of Cortes, and thousands of whales from the whole world had come to our encounter. It was after that dream that I realized that our relationship, if it could be called that, would not work because sooner or later, my conscience would disturb me for having separated you from your wife and daughter. A situation of this type was also not fair for my boyfriend, Jorge. Deep down, I knew that the moment would come when I wouldn't know what to do because I'm sure that I would never stop loving Jorge.

"Within the first couple of weeks, when I became conscious of this situation, I was depressed and I was very sad. I didn't want you to notice any of this. Then, when I began to feel a little bit better, I thought that if you were happily married, and I also was happily engaged, then our ways at some moment were going to separate. I also considered that it would be very difficult for me to continue working with you if our relationship continued in the direction it had taken. Also, I think that neither of us would be willing to change it. You and I would first begin to live the joy and the emotion of being lovers. Then, once things and affections that had been blended within us ended adjusting and calming down, everything would begin to be different and who knows what would happen then. Also, I was afraid that you would come to despise me if our relationship didn't work.

"There's only left to say that, in these days, I will begin another stage in my life, and by this letter, I wish to thank you for how happy you made me feel the whole time in which we were real workmates. I keep with much love all the signs of affection that you showed me. Thank you, for everything, Sir. I send you a kiss and I hope it lasts forever. I will never forget you,

"Patty."

I finished reading the letter and I felt a great nuisance in my whole body. I wanted to get up from the chair where I was sitting but couldn't. I was completely invaded by reluctance. Then, after keeping Patty's letter in my hands without reading it, I began to react. What could I reproach her? I tried to remember and, indeed, I would see her in such and such occasion being on the watch for the work and, also, of me. The physical attraction had been a screen for me to forget the absurd demands of useless or scarce value work that she and I had to do to meet the demands of an overbearing boss like Carlos.

"Damn it! I'm going to miss Patty," I thought completely discouraged, a little before I got my strength together to get up from the chair and go upstairs to my office.

While I was slowly going to my cubicle, I realized that internally, I knew that Patty's absence was going to affect me a great deal, and that, thanks to her, I had stopped seeing Carlos as a despot and good-for-nothing boss. Both of us always got down to work and got all the pending matters efficiently out on time. Now, coming to my mind were the times when I saw Carlos shouting at office people from the entrance door of the Association because someone had done something, which even if it was well done, he had not liked. I also began to remember in detail the moments in which Carlos treated the office members as useless and humiliated them. Today he humiliated the employees of the marketing team of the firm; tomorrow, those of the accounting department; and the day after tomorrow, any one of the others who work at the Association.

In those days, Patty represented many things to me. Among them, she was the illusion of being in an agreeable job where the fits, arrogant remarks, and even the threats of the boss aren't relevant, because one meets one's obligations and one has valid motivating interests, and what one does makes sense.

I also remember when I was going upstairs to go to my office, I was mentally grateful to Patty, with my whole heart, for the nice gestures she always showed me. At that moment, I realized that she had been a magnificent workmate and work friend, and I was sure that, regardless of her beauty and appeal, I would never have a friend like that in the office again.

"Give me Patty or give me electroshocks," I told myself with a certain sadness as I neared my desk. I smiled because I was sure that no electroshock, no matter how intense, would ever substitute Patty.

VI
Rafa, my Boss

When I met Rafael many years ago, I thought that they were introducing me to a famous boxer from Mexico City. Due to his physical shape, it seemed like Rafael spent his mornings in one of the gyms of *La Doctores*, a neighborhood known for being the breeding ground of pugilists, the kind that sooner or later win a boxing world title. There he was. The thing was to remember what I had imagined on that occasion: Rafael, in shorts, practicing his boxing routines with his shadow constantly, mercilessly hitting his assistants of combat practice and sweating profusely through each of his, if not infinite, at least innumerable pores. Rafael's smile was the magnet that attracted a multitude of young men who considered him an idol, a role model.

Years later, here in the office, I only had to close my eyes and see his speed. One, two, three, and Rafael was already walking, with quick foot movements toward an invisible enemy. Before having thrown his combination of blows, he had dodged, by bending his waist, a pair of hypothetical punches. One, two, three, and now Rafael was using one of those combinations of blows that had made him famous: first, a quick jab on the right, followed by a potent hook on the left, as the precursor of a right straight loaded with dynamite. All these routines and movements were always executed by Rafael at the gym and the office with precision, neatness, and excellent synchronization. This would bring his admirers to always acclaim him with an unending series of cheers. For Rafael, this shouting was a sweet song that encouraged him to continue to be the number one in his category. What's more, he always liked to be called, by way of a nickname, "The Number One." He was number one, the invincible, and best of everything, the champion. That was Rafa. Of humble origin, who was going to remember that, before he became famous, he lived huddled in a vicinity destined to oblivion, in addition to being filthy and foul-smelling, and that he attacked all his neighbors with cruelty, just to have fun? Who would remember that the first rival that he knocked out in his career was Rosa, his longtime girlfriend, when he had been drinking in excess during a *quinceañera* party, and she had started flirting with some unknown guys from the nearest table when Rafael got up staggering to run to the toilet in urgency? The thing is that champions like Rafa, which is more than the truth, don't urinate anywhere nor are they born just anywhere. Little by little, they are forged into shape on the street, with the empty Bacardi bottles and many other labels, by continuously ingesting tequilas and Caguama beers, and also by the fights that irremediably surge on the street. That had been the University of Life from which Rafael had graduated, with honors, much before having started the school year that took him to obtain his degree in Hits, Shouts, and Blows.

Indeed, I just had to close my eyes to see Rafael, not in his office, but at one of those Night Clubs in the Guerrero neighborhood, drinking a lot of rum with coke to wane his thirst, to relax, and smiling at Rosa, who was sitting next to him with the powerful right hand of the champion on her legs—she, flirtatious; he, ugly and defiant with his toad face. Yeah, wanting it or not, Rafael, as an office worker or a boxer, looked like a toad with that ugly face of his, fat with bulging eyes, almost pop-eyed. Yeah, he of the Bacardi bottle, the old time's prizefighter, idolized by the multitudes and he of the semi-deformed face was no one but Rafael, the great dancer of the main cabarets and night places of San Juan de Letran and Izazaga. Thus, one, two, three steps this way, and one, two, three steps that way, it was how Rafa moved on the dance floor. Just from seeing him dance, one would know how he had been able to take an important and firm step toward boxing. Who the heck in the office would want to be knocked out in a "one, two, three" rhythm of cha-cha-cha or mambo?

On the other hand, something inside was telling me that I should remember every detail of the occasion in which I saw Rafael for the first time. My mind was telling me that when I was introduced to him, he had shaken my hand with much force, and I realized that his hand was a bit deformed. Even though now, at a later moment and different time in my work life, in his office, his aspect was completely challenging, I remembered entirely the most minimal details and thoughts that I had the moment I met him. It was enough to blink to once again see his smile, intended to be frank and even friendly. Unfortunately for his aspect, his denture was in a bad condition, and a broken tooth could be seen.

The pat he gave me on the shoulder on that occasion made me see him smile in the boxing ring. His gloves were untied and he was wearing his gala shorts and his phosphorescent robe. The public was applauding him euphorically and vibrantly. The loudspeakers were heard to be saying mechanically and monotonously, although respectfully:

"On this corner is the number one pugilist in his weight, the invincible and formidable Rafael 'The Toad' Montes, of 89 kilos and 1.73 meters high."

Immediately after, came to my mind the shouting by the public as a sign of affection for the champion. Rafael, on his part, circumscribed himself to just smile, raised his arms, and went to the center of the combat ring. Rosa, his girlfriend, was sending him kisses from the third row and shouted at him,

"You are the number one, Rafa, 'The Number One.'"

His fans, his soul followers, supported him and advised him. They shouted as loud as possible,

"Don't let your opponent come near you, Rafa. Finish him up right away. Don't let him reach the fifth round, Rafa. You can do it. Demolish him. Kill him with blows, if necessary, champion. Don't forget the right. Use your murderous right, Rafa, you who are 'The Number One.'"

Then, another deafening shouting took place and the lights of the reflectors increased their power until they were blinding. At that moment, Rafa went to the center of the ring seeking an ephemeral opponent to come out of the rows of the appreciable public. With his scrutinizing look of courageous and cowards, and full of hate, he examined all those present to detect who would even dare to hold his look for just a few seconds.

Indeed, that was the Rafael that I had in mind when I met him, and he was the same who was about to get up from his desk in the middle of a fit of rage. Who would have imagined this? The boss, according to what Bertha, the secretary, said, had assaulted her. No, it wasn't possible for such atrocities to happen at an office, and much less in a Development Bank. It was just something to be reported, and the end of the matter. The boss, that is Rafa, would be fired as per Bertha's logic. But she, in the end, never did anything, and everything remained the same, except that, now, Bertha held a terrible grudge against Rafael. Her great consolation was having told him, totally indignant, seconds before she burst out crying,

"Forgive me, but you behave like a cold-blooded boxer."

We all heard Rafael's clamorous guffaws when Bertha stopped talking. It seemed that the comparison had pleased him and even made him happy for a few instants. We all at the office felt that, on this occasion, Rafael had laughed at Bertha and each one of us. Maybe, some of us had a foreboding that something disagreeable could happen to us in the future.

"Hysterical secretaries," Rafael told me once I was in his office. It seemed that deep down, he wanted to minimize the importance of the incident that he had had with Bertha.

After two or three weeks, there was an argument with the messenger. Another foolish act. First, there were shouts and even a shove inside his private office. What had happened, as per Rafael's version, was that Victor didn't want to recognize and, obviously pay, for a scratch that he had caused on Rafael's car. According to Rafa, Victor had damaged his car on purpose.

"It's not possible to have a boss like that," Bertha said annoyed, heated, and giving us to understand that she had put herself in Victor's shoes during the whole misunderstanding.

"It's denigrating," Bertha added with a broken voice and eyes full of tears. She crossed her arms and began to fervently wish that Rafael would rot soon.

Victor, for his part, agreed with her. Deep down, this gesture of solidarity by Bertha for Victor was as if she had come near him and given him the sincerest and heartfelt embrace of his life. But, what could he do? For Victor, to go to the

Labor Relations Department or the Personnel Department was equivalent to being left without a job. Who was going to be right: the intelligent and reliable boss or the dumb and problematic subordinate?

These facts also made Rafael become the champion of the office. He now had in his private account two knockouts: Bertha and Victor, both in the first round. That's being "The Number One." The other members of the Accounting Department never thought about acclaiming our pugilist or encouraging him. Rather, we all thought of developing work strategies to avoid him. One way or another, when the workday began, all of us at the office, instead of looking at Rafael when we greeted him with certain fear, always set our look on his fists. At that moment, something would darken inside each one of us. We were, in short, a sad public, listless, and that only wished that the night boxing function would end to go home to rest and forget for some hours that the office existed, and to recall those joyful and carefree times when Rafael hadn't yet come to work at the bank.

"Javier," I remember him saying to me in an energetic tone of voice, "please come into my cubicle."

"Whatever you wish, champion," I thought about telling him. "I'll be there with you in a second," was what I only answered him.

From Rafael's attitude and the tone of his voice, surely problems were waiting for me in his office due to some work matter. Once I entered his private office, he began to complain about the reason why I hadn't informed him of a meeting of the Board of Directors.

"Sure I did. I made a note of it in your agenda," I told him.

"Don't think you can fool me," he answered me, shouting at the same time that his face seemed to enlarge and his eyes were bloating.

"Nobody shouts at me," I told myself.

While trying to calm me down, I showed him that in his agenda, that meeting was noted down in my handwriting. Next to my note, Rafael had written down, *Javier says that it is necessary to have the profit-and-loss statement. Consult.*

"Look Javier, I'm not your jeer," he told me in a threatening tone and pushed toward me his agenda, with a certain air of contempt.

"Nor am I yours," I answered, losing my temper.

At that moment, I saw that Rafael had been transformed. Under his suit, he was wearing his boxing uniform. In less than one second, he pulled out his gloves from the drawer and began to challenge me with his look. I was aware that his eyes indicated hate and a fervent wish to see me defeated and bleeding at his feet. On that occasion, as opposed to those before, there was no public, no ovations, no shouting, but a tense and threatening silence, accompanied by a blinding light. I could see how he got up agilely from his chair and attacked me with his right hand. I tried to dodge his blow, but I couldn't do it on time. Before partially seeing how his face quivered and became angry with the first punch that I gave him, I could hear that he shouted at me joyfully:

"You stupid! You don't know who you're dealing with!"

A fraction of a second later, with his left hand, he hurled at my eyes the boiling contents of his coffee cup. Without knowing it, I found myself amid the shouting and the blinding lights: facing me was "The Number One." I felt sure that I would win the fight. My hate grew as my eyes burned, the blows hurt me and I recalled his guffaws full of jeer and contempt.